TREES IN BRITAIN

Aspen glade with bluebells at Headley

TREES IN BRITAIN
AN ILLUSTRATED GUIDE

BRIAN GRIMES and ERIC HERBERT

Drawings by Syd Lewis

Webb & Bower
MICHAEL JOSEPH

First published in Great Britain 1988 by
Webb & Bower (Publishers) Limited
9 Colleton Crescent, Exeter, Devon EX2 4BY
in association with Michael Joseph Limited
27 Wright's Lane, London W8 5TZ

Designed by Peter Wrigley

Production by Nick Facer/Rob Kendrew

British Library Cataloguing in Publication Data

Grimes, Brian
Trees in Britain: an illustrated guide.
1.Great Britain. Trees
I.Title   II.Herbert, Eric
582.160941
ISBN   0–86350–256–3

Typeset in Great Britain by Keyspools Limited, Golborne,
Lancashire

Colour and mono reproduction by Peninsular Repro Service
Limited, Exeter, Devon

Printed and bound in Italy by New Interlitho SpA, Milan

CONTENTS

PREFACE

Although there are a number of informative and beautifully illustrated books on trees, we felt that there was a need for a book concerned principally with the evolution of native trees in Britain and with the most important introduced trees. This book contains a descriptive text on individual species, together with colour photographs and line drawings. It also deals with the evolution of trees, and highlights some of the ecological, social and economic benefits they bring to our countryside. It ends with a discussion of the decline of tree cover in recent decades, and measures which can be taken to halt it.

To some extent the storm which swept through south-east England on 16 October 1987 has been the catalyst for this book. This area is very rich in parks and famous landscaped gardens. Many of their rare trees have been destroyed, trees that had been brought to this country by those intrepid plant hunters of one or two centuries ago. Several of these rare trees were photographed during the preparation of this book and have since become victims of the storm. They have been included with short descriptions and photographs in the section devoted to the storm, for both of our homes were in the direct line of the storm, and so later that morning we were able to begin covering photographically many of the most devastated areas. A selection of these photographs also appears in the section on the storm, together with a report.

The decline of trees is not, of course, just a national problem. It is global and, hence, we have decided to devote a section of this book to the increasingly critical situation worldwide. In particular we have given space to the desperate predicament in which the world's most valuable and, at the same time, most threatened ecosystems, the tropical rain forests, find themselves.

A Cedar of Lebanon: trees become well-known, majestic landmarks in the British landscape.

6

FOREWORD

by J Morton Boyd, CBE, DSc, PhD, FRSE

The history of land use in Britain in the last 5000 years has been that of continuous deforestation in the face of advancing agriculture and industrial development. The ecological consequences of this are obvious everywhere today, but the psychological consequences are less so. In the inherited memory of the British people, there is no recall of the natural forest, which is such a strong force among Scandinavians, Bavarians and Canadians, and which plays such a great part in the formulation of their national character. Relict traditions of the native forest people probably still survive, where stands of old native trees persist in the New Forest, Forest of Dean and other extensive ancient semi-natural woods in England and Wales, and in the native pine woods of the Spey and Dee Valleys in Scotland. However, there is a strong innate sentiment in the people as a whole for the charm of woodlands and the beauty of trees – a gut-feeling against the felling of old trees and in favour of the planting of more native species.

Native species are important in conservation, but they are a minor part of our present day inheritance of trees in Britain. The introduction of alien species by man since Roman times has resulted in a long inventory of trees which are grown for commercial and decorative purposes. Sylviculture has been an art as well as a science. Exotic spruces, pines, larches and firs provide fine crops of timber in different parts of the country, and our woodlands, parks and gardens are enhanced by an array of ornamental maples, sycamores, cherries, cedars, poplars and chestnuts – to mention but a few. Each contributes its shape, colour, and texture to the seasonal kaleidoscope of the lowland countryside. Many of the exotic conifers used in commercial forestry have a bad reputation from a fault which is not their own. They are grown in thick stands, become tall and spindly, and are felled in their youth. The same species grown in the wild, or within a park woodland, to old age, will be elegant of shape and a complement to the landscape. While many of these exotics do not have as many species of fauna and flora living on them as do the native oak, ash, birch and willow, they nevertheless make a great contribution to the conservation of woodland habitat in the British countryside. Sycamore has the reputation of an aggressive colonizer and is disliked for its sticky drippings of honey-dew, on the other hand it is a most shapely and colourful tree which produces good timber, enhances many a bleak north country farm, and grows on the exposed north-western seaboard where few other trees can survive.

Nature conservation has come increasingly from the countryside into the towns and cities. The die-back of the inner cities, the creation of New Towns and Garden Cities, and the inception of green-belt planning strategies have all helped to concentrate the public mind on the use of trees in the built environment, as a medium in landscape design. Nothing relieves better the hard texture of the concrete and built stone, than a gentle cumulus of foliage; or the angularity of walls, roofs, pillars and windows, than the curves of canopy in sunlight and shadow; or the unchanging face of street and square, than the seasonal change from leaf-spread, to fall, to the stark winter garb of the broadleaved trees. The same can be said for motorways, where the growing of trees is producing fresh woodland vistas for the traveller as part of a new linear habitat throughout the country, possessing its own quota of flora and fauna.

Our world is full of trees of many kinds, which silently serve us both day and night in so many ways, yet we do not know them nearly well enough to appreciate the vital role which they play in our lives. In this book the authors have given vivid profiles of British trees which will quicken the minds and hearts of the British people to what is one of their most valuable natural resources.

INTRODUCTION

On 16 October 1987, in the early hours of the morning, winds of hurricane force struck the south east of England. This catastrophe altered the entire character of the landscape, perhaps irrevocably, within two hours. It has been estimated that 15,000,000 trees were destroyed, over 2,000,000 in Kent alone.

We live in an age which has accustomed us to stories of environmental destruction on a grand scale. It is, as often as not, man-made, or its impact is greatly increased by man-made factors, and it happens usually in other parts of the world. In Britain, too, we have become accustomed to the idea that our own landscape is under threat from industrial pollution, development and modern agricultural methods. However, despite the fact that during the twentieth century we have been more profligate with our countryside than in any other, we are too ready to perceive these forces as relatively gradual ones, which can, with efficient management, be halted and reversed with time.

The magnitude of the storm served as a shock reminder that our landscape is in fact as fragile as any in the world. The force of the wind combined with the great age of many of our countryside trees destroyed large parts of our landscape. The foresight of our forebears in the late eighteenth and in the nineteenth centuries in planting trees has not been matched by anything comparable in this century, and our remaining legacy of trees is an ageing and vulnerable one. Today only eight per cent of our land is covered with trees, one of the smallest percentages in Europe. Moreover, the steadily increasing proportion of exotic conifers planted conceals the true extent of the decline of native broad-leaved woodlands, with their rich associations of plants and animals.

There are, however, some causes for cautious optimism. For example, the impending release of land from agricultural use, and the recently introduced grants for broadleaved tree planting, could mark a turning point in the decline of our native trees.

There is no doubt that the British landscape holds a special place in the hearts of its people. Particularly since the eighteenth century, when the national love affair with the beauties of nature really took a hold, not only artists and writers but the British people at large have sought and found inspiration in it.

As anyone who has travelled in recent years through parts of East Anglia will know, the character of the landscape is derived in large part from the trees and other vegetation which grow upon it. What we see there today is no longer the landscape of Constable. For the British, a feeling of belonging is intimately bound up with a feeling for the countryside. Unfortunately, the landscape of Constable has not been replaced with anything that might inspire equivalent feelings of belonging – a prairie, stripped of its varied vegetation, provides for us a depressing and spiritually alienating experience.

This national feeling for the countryside was most immediately expressed in the aftermath of the storm. Perfect strangers would approach you in the street, on the downs or in woodlands, sometimes with tears in their eyes, and their voices filled with emotion as they recalled with sadness the destruction of their favourite trees or the loss of some sylvan landscape.

Trees add greatly to the quality of our lives, whether they are admired displaying their individual magnificence in one of Britain's famous gardens, as part of native woodlands, or relieving the harsh lines of our towns and cities.

However, the aesthetic imperative is by no means the only one to which we ought to pay heed. There are other reasons, perhaps even more compelling, why we ought to look after our trees and woodlands as part of a concerted effort to maintain the varied landscape of Britain. These reasons have to do with the long term economic viability of the countryside – with the preservation of habitat and soils. These are the preconditions for the sustainability of food production and the maintenance of genetic diversity.

1 : THE LIVING TREE

Trees are the most dominant vegetation on Earth. They are also astonishingly diverse, 'tree' being the general term given to the woody members of many plant families. Some can grow to over 100m (330ft) high while others, by contrast, can be trained as bonsai trees measuring only a few centimetres' (inches). The oldest living thing is a tree – the Bristlecone Pine, a native of Colorado and Utah, some specimens of which have lived for at least 5000 years.

Trees and shrubs are woody perennials. The trunk or bole, branches and twigs provide a spreading framework for the attachment of the leaves, which are thus optimally disposed to absorb sunlight. The leaves are, in essence, small solar cells which derive energy from the sunlight to power the tree's life processes and produce the raw materials necessary for its growth. This chemical process is called photosynthesis.

Trees and shrubs have a considerable advantage over non-woody plants such as herbs and grasses. Non-woody plants die off annually or biennially and renew themselves by seeding, and hence do not attain a great age.

THE STRUCTURE AND LIFE PROCESSES OF A TREE

The wood

Wood is entirely the product of the cambium, which is the live generative membrane, a mere one cell thick, that surrounds the entire tree, just below the bark, to the finer extremities of the roots and twigs, where it merges with the multiplying cells at the growing points of the root and twig tips.

In broadleaved trees, the sapwood primarily consists of long narrow tube-cells of cellulose, named tracheary elements. These are slender and tapering and are joined one to another in series. They channel the rising sap from the roots to the leaves. Sandwiched between these tubes is a dense packing of long fibrous cells of cellulose. At an earlier stage, this dense complex of interlocking cells is impregnated with lignin, which bestows on it its woody quality and strength.

In the interstitial spaces is a complex of thin-walled parenchyma cells impregnated with starch. Vertical bands of these cells are concentrated in the medullary rays, which when seen in cross-section are dark radial lines. The hardest and most durable wood is located in the core of the tree. It is biologically dead and inert, serving as a disposal area for waste products, in particular tannin, which often, but not invariably, stains the wood a dark reddish colour, as well as acting as a preservative.

In conifers or softwoods, the sapwood's texture is different. The bore of the tube-cells, or tracheids, is finer and the walls thicker and reinforced with spirals of lignin. The long fibrous cells are largely incorporated into the walls of the tracheids. They are not continuous sap channels as in broadleaved trees, but the rising sap passes from cell to cell through perforations in the walls of the tightly packed overlapping ends of the tracheids.

In both broadleaved trees and conifers, annual rings are visible on a cross-section, for example a sawn trunk. Each ring represents one year's growth and increase in girth. In some species, including oak and ash, the spring growth is represented by a wider, more light in colour, and more porous band; in autumn wood by a narrower darker band.

Growth

Tree growth varies throughout the year and many of the temperate zone trees become dormant during the winter. Upward growth is achieved by means of terminal buds, which are the embryo shoots. The side buds of a shoot or branch are the embryo leaves or flower buds.

At the beginning of the growing season the cambium cells separate to produce new cells, some becoming xylem or wood cells, and the others becoming phloem. The outward growth of the girth of the trunk and branches is the result of the annual addition to the sapwood, generated from the cambium.

Circulation

The sap is drawn upwards into the leaves from the roots through the sapwood (or xylem) inside the cambium. The sap containing the nutrients from the leaves is conveyed through the bast (or phloem) and the pores in the cambium to all the woody parts of the tree. It requires great energy to raise a column of liquid from the roots to the highest leaves of a tree. It is now considered that the evaporation of transpiring water from the leaves is sufficient to maintain an unbroken column of sap moving upwards. Once started, the process is continuous.

Twigs and branches

The twigs are the youngest growth of the tree apart from the cambium growth of the trunk. With the leaves they produce and support, they form the outer shell or canopy of the tree's crown, where the leaves can absorb the energy from the sun to synthesize carbohydrates or sugars. In winter twigs carry the buds for the following spring's new growth. The colouring of the twigs and buds in many species is an aid to identification in the absence of leaves.

The terminal bud or buds of a twig contain the embryo shoot and the folded new leaves for emergence in spring. The side buds below are leaf or flower buds, which develop in the axils of the leaf scars. They occur at regular intervals along the twig in opposite pairs, or singly or alternately, according to the species.

In many trees, including Ash and Horse Chestnut, conspicuous ring scars occur at intervals along the twig, fading out towards the older wood. They mark the beginning and end of a year's growth. In older wood, from the second year onwards, some side shoots develop shoots of their own, and they start new branches. The majority of twigs produced die off and fall to the ground. If this did not happen the interior of dense crowns would become a tangle of useless foliage.

The roots

Water and minerals needed by the tree are absorbed through the root hairs, the very delicate filaments clustered near the extremities of the rootlets. The delicate outer covering of the hairs is a semipermeable membrane that allows water and dissolved minerals to filter selectively through, by the process known as osmosis: the solution in the soil being stronger than that in the root hairs, the solution passes through into the hairs in order to equalize strengths.

Root symbiosis

The rootlets of most trees have a symbiotic relationship with fungus in the soil. This fungus manufactures the minerals required by the tree and the tree provides the sugars needed by the fungus. For this reason it is important that great care is taken when transplanting trees and shrubs not to disturb the soil round the root mass.

The leaves

Most broadleaved trees keep their leaves for about six months, apart from a few exceptions such as the Holly, which is evergreen, having a waxy cuticle to protect its leaves from frost. The flattened form of the leaf gives it a large surface to enable it to absorb carbon dioxide from the air and it attains a position which is most advantageous to catching the rays of the sun, so enabling it to carry out its chemical function of photosynthesis. Leaves also draw up dissolved minerals from the soil via the roots.

The epidermis, or outer layer, of the leaf, which usually has a well-developed cuticle, often has a fine layer of wax to prevent excessive loss of water. Spreading veins allow the flow of solutions to the spongy cells and also support the leaf tissue.

Why do leaves have such varied forms and arrangements? It is possibly an adaptation to obtain as much sunlight as possible, especially where the number of sunlight hours is limited.

The leaves of deciduous trees fall at the end of the growing season, leaving the stems bare until the following spring. Before the leaf falls a layer of cork forms across the base of the petiole, to protect the stem once the leaf has gone. The leaf

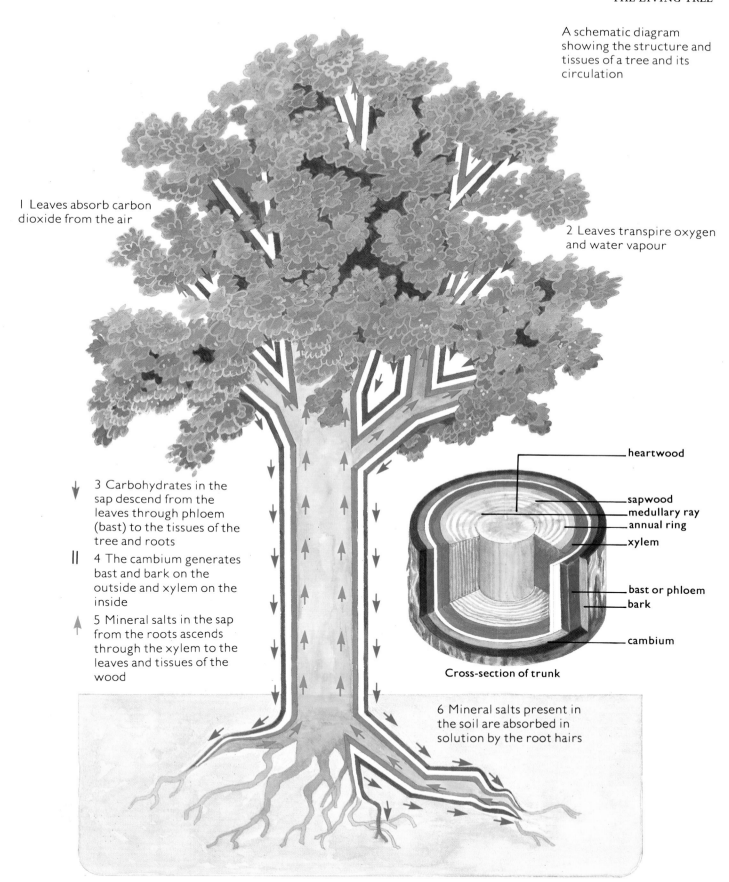

A schematic diagram
showing the structure and
tissues of a tree and its
circulation

1 Leaves absorb carbon
dioxide from the air

2 Leaves transpire oxygen
and water vapour

↓ 3 Carbohydrates in the
sap descend from the
leaves through phloem
(bast) to the tissues of the
tree and roots

‖ 4 The cambium generates
bast and bark on the
outside and xylem on the
inside

↑ 5 Mineral salts in the sap
from the roots ascends
through the xylem to the
leaves and tissues of the
wood

6 Mineral salts present in
the soil are absorbed in
solution by the root hairs

heartwood

sapwood
medullary ray
annual ring
xylem

bast or phloem
bark

cambium

Cross-section of trunk

fall is determined by a combination of the interruption or failure of the water supply, the length of daylight, and the temperature. (A severe frost at any time will kill the leaves of broadleaved trees.) The new leaves will not begin to grow until the daylight increases the following spring.

In autumn the leaves are at their most colourful. This colouring varies within different species. Ageing of a leaf is not always consistent over the whole of the leaf, so that the leaf can vary in coloration. If cartenoid pigments are present within the leaf then it will turn a yellowish colour. In beeches and aspens if tannin is also present a bright golden yellow often results. The most colourful of leaves, those of the maples, contain an excess of sugars, resulting in vivid purples and reds.

Photosynthesis and nutrition

The tree, in common with all green plants, derives energy from sunlight to fuel its life processes. It uses the energy so captured to make the raw materials that it needs from the carbon dioxide in the atmosphere and the water and minerals conducted upwards from the soil.

The initial chemical process occurs within the leaves, which are ideally designed for penetration by sunlight. The green pigment of leaves, chlorophyll, combines carbon dioxide and water with the energy from sunlight, to synthesize carbohydrates or sugars. Oxygen is given off into the atmosphere as a by-product – but only during the hours of daylight, as photosynthesis is obviously suspended during darkness.

Mineral salts are necessary for the proteins that develop the tissues of the tree and ascend through the sapwood from the soil to the leaves where the proteins needed by the leaves and other tissues are synthesized. The dissolved mineral salts and the immediate products, amino acids, are conducted downwards through the phloem to all other parts of the tree.

Nutritional reserves are stored in the heartwood and medullary rays, especially during winter after the leaves have been shed and the chlorophyll has been withdrawn into the tree.

Respiration and excretion

Respiration is a breathing process by which foods are broken down within a cell, with some of the energy being released into the metabolic system of the cell. There are no special respiratory organs in plants, but the absorption of oxygen is most rapid in parts of the plant where the katabolic processes (the breaking down of complex substances into simpler substances) are most active, eg leaves, growing shoots and germinating seeds. Many different substances are respired but glucose is the most typical.

Oxygen enters the plant through stomata or lenticels, and passes in solution into the cells through the cell walls. Respiration in green plants (those containing chlorophyll) is concealed during daylight due to the activity of carbon-assimilation. Respiration occurs over the whole of the plant and oxygen passes into the plant and carbon dioxide is given off. In the process of photosynthesis, when only the aerial green parts are active in the production of food, carbon dioxide is assimilated from the atmosphere and oxygen is given off.

Reproduction

This is accomplished by various means, according to the type of plant. The (male) pollen in most plants consists of loose dusty powder, made up of large numbers of minute grains. In order for the seed to be produced the pollen grains must be transferred to the (female) stigma, either of the same flower or another flower of the same species. In self-pollinating flowers the pollen grains are transferred from the anthers to the stigma of the same flower. In cross-pollination they are either transferred by insects or wind to another flower of the same plant or another plant of the same species.

Flowers

The function of flowers is essentially to produce seeds and fruit, and their various parts have been specially adapted to perform that task. The flowers' most important organs are the pollen sacs and the ovules, which are concerned with the production of seeds. These organs may be developed on the floral leaves or in the axes of the flowers. They correspond to the spores of the lower plants.

The egg of a conifer is naked and situated on a bract (a modified leaf) between the scales of the cones. A male sperm (pollen grain) merely alights on the egg to obtain fertilization. In most conifers the sexes are separate but on the same tree, and the transfer of pollen can be by insects or the wind. The eggs of broadleaved trees, in contrast, are protected by ovaries and the sperm (pollen grain) must penetrate the ovary to fertilize the egg.

Seeds and fruits

A fruit is the ripe seed inside its protective ovary. It is only the true flowering plants, the Angiosperm division of the plant kingdom, which produce fruit.

Conifers developed before ovaries evolved in plants, and hence do not produce fruit. Their seeds develop on the cones and are shed without any covering. By contrast, broadleaved trees and shrubs (the arboreal form of Angiosperms) have evolved diverse forms of covering to protect their seeds and to aid their dispersal. These coverings vary from dry capsules to fleshy and juicy ones. Those now described will refer only to trees.

The fruits most commonly seen are named 'achenes'. They are dry fruits which do not split open to release their seed, but are shed complete with the seed inside. The dry casing is the ovary. One form of achene is the 'samara', in which the ovary is a leathery capsule extended into a wing to aid wind dispersal. Maples, ash, hornbeam, and the tree of heaven are all examples of trees which produce these. Another form of achene is the nut, in which the single seed or kernel is protected within a hard woody shell, as in the hazelnut, or within a horny leathery pellicle, as in oaks (acorns), horse chestnuts, chestnuts and beeches. In the latter three there are two or three nuts, each in its own ovary or carpel, and they are all encased together in a spiny husk, a derived form of the calyx. The downy seeds of willows and the winged seeds of birches are small forms of achenes.

In magnolias the seeds are ejected naked from the ovaries, which are clustered on a central cone of the flower. These fruits are termed dehiscent (which means gaping or bursting open) and the ovaries remain on the tree. The pea-like nodes of the Judas Tree and the Laburnum are single carpel fruits, containing a string of seeds; the peas are ejected by the splitting and twisting of the dry two-valved pod.

Succulent fruits evolved in order to attract birds and animals, through the alimentary canals of which their seeds have come to be dispersed. The most common succulent fruits are the drupes. Drupes are stone fruits, and are found on, for example, hawthorns, cherries, and plums, among others. The seed or kernel is contained in a hard stony casing which is surrounded by a juicy pulp.

Other succulent fruits, for example of the Rowan and other members of the genus Sorbus, are berries. Berries are small and pulpy and contain more than one seed. Another succulent fruit is the 'pome', which usually comprises five carpels, each containing a seed and each protected by a horny compartment of the core. The pulp consists of a thick calyx. Apples are pomes.

Suckers

Some trees reproduce via this vegetative method. They grow underground branches and runners which then grow upwards and develop roots and aerial shoots, so a clone is formed because the shoots are genetically identical. This form of reproduction is common in the Willow family.

CLASSIFICATION

There is an infinite variety of form represented in the Plant Kingdom. The work of the taxonomist is to organize the knowledge of the diversity and variability among organisms into a system of classification which reflects not only their evolutionary origin, but also their similarities and differences. This classification is based upon the various methods of plant reproduction that have evolved over the

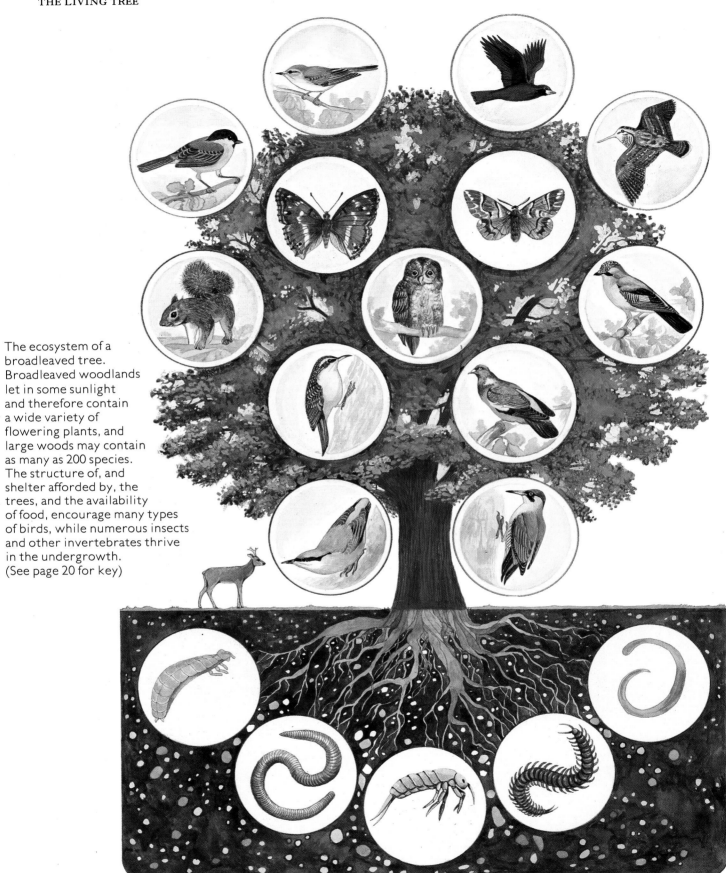

The ecosystem of a broadleaved tree. Broadleaved woodlands let in some sunlight and therefore contain a wide variety of flowering plants, and large woods may contain as many as 200 species. The structure of, and shelter afforded by, the trees, and the availability of food, encourage many types of birds, while numerous insects and other invertebrates thrive in the undergrowth. (See page 20 for key)

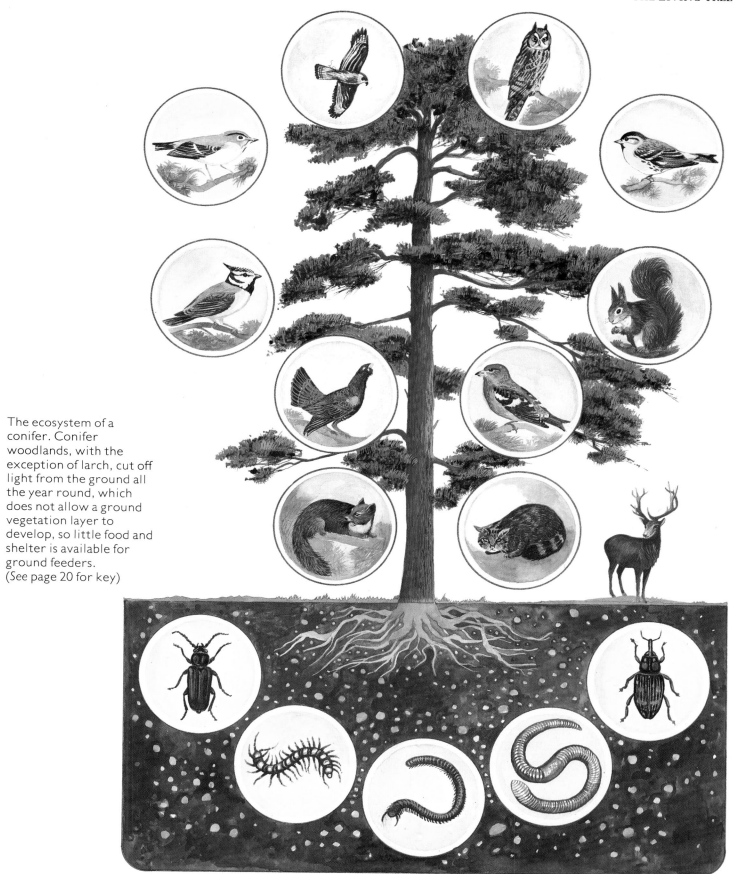

The ecosystem of a conifer. Conifer woodlands, with the exception of larch, cut off light from the ground all the year round, which does not allow a ground vegetation layer to develop, so little food and shelter is available for ground feeders.
(*See page 20 for key*)

THE PLANT KINGDOM

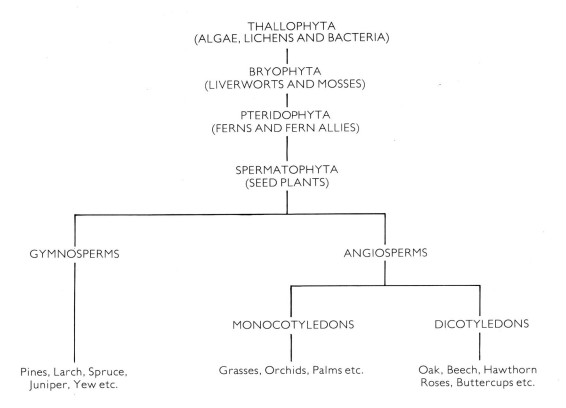

THALLOPHYTA
(ALGAE, LICHENS AND BACTERIA)

BRYOPHYTA
(LIVERWORTS AND MOSSES)

PTERIDOPHYTA
(FERNS AND FERN ALLIES)

SPERMATOPHYTA
(SEED PLANTS)

GYMNOSPERMS

ANGIOSPERMS

MONOCOTYLEDONS

DICOTYLEDONS

Pines, Larch, Spruce, Juniper, Yew etc.

Grasses, Orchids, Palms etc.

Oak, Beech, Hawthorn Roses, Buttercups etc.

last 500,000,000 years. The four main groups of the Plant Kingdom, together with the more important sub-divisions, are shown above.

The Thallophyta include:

i the Schizomycetes, commonly known as Bacteria

ii the Algae, including seaweeds and aquatic ferns

iii Fungi, including moulds and toadstools

The Pteridophyta or Vascular Cryptograms include ferns, horsetails and club-mosses

The Spermaphyta or Seed Plants include the Gymnosperms and the typical flowering plants, the Angiosperms

The vascular system consists of tissues which enable the plant to transfer nutrients rapidly lengthwise throughout its structure. Typical vascular tissue is found only in Vascular Cryptograms and flowering plants.

Generic and specific nomenclature

The classification of plants was pioneered by Carl Linnaeus, the great Swedish botanist (1707–78). He proposed that the naming of all living things should be systematized by grouping them according to common characteristics (a genus). The members (or species) within each group (or genus) would then be further subdivided and given their own specific names, to give two names each. For example, maples are given the generic name of *Acer*, and the Norway Maple is given the specific name *platanoides*, thus *Acer platanoides*. Latin, the language of scholarship, with an international currency and acceptability, was adopted as the vehicle for this system.

Infra-specific nomenclature

The two part names, followed by the names of the first persons to describe the plant (which are not given in this book), are the basic units of the classification of trees and plants, but are also divisible into sub-species, now called varieties. These varieties are mainly geographical forms derived from a common stock. Each is given a third name prefixed by the abbreviation 'var.'. The first time a species is recognized and described, it is called a 'type' and does not necessarily represent the ancestral stock. For example, the Austrian Pine *Pinus nigra* var. *nigra* was the first Black Pine to be described and is therefore the 'type' of the species.

The naming of hybrid trees

Most hybrids, both arising in the wild and produced by man, are crosses between species of the same genus. This is usually signified by an 'X' in front of the assigned name for the hybrid. For example, the Common Lime is *Tilia X europaea* (syn. *T vulgaris*) and the Hybrid Larch, a cross between the European and the Japanese Larch, is *Larix X eurolepis*.

TYPES OF TREE AND THEIR DISTRIBUTION

Naked seeds and hidden seeds

In the plant group, the Angiosperms ('hidden seeds'), to which all the broad-leaved trees belong, the ovule (the egg) is contained within a protective ovary. The second group, the Gymnosperms ('naked seeds'), by contrast, do not have their ovules contained within a protective ovary. Instead, they are freely attached to the cone scale without a protective cover. Gymnosperms include, most importantly, the conifers. Angiosperms are conveniently referred to as the typical flowering plants. As such, they form the most recently evolved division of plants. Their ancestry can be traced by fossil evidence to the mid-Jurassic period 160–170,000,000 years ago.

Angiosperms are divided into two groups. The first, the Monocotyledons, which includes grasses, bamboos and palms, is so called because there is only one cotyledon, or seed leaf. The structure of the tissue and the mode of growth is different from that of the second group, the Dicotyledons.

Dicotyledons are the typical flowering plants and the most successful, diverse and evolutionarily advanced form of plant life. Two seed leaves are present in the early seedlings and, in some species of trees, including the Oak and the Horse Chestnut, they remain within the seed until the food is consumed. In Beech, they are fused into one leaf.

Gymnosperm trees are evolutionarily more ancient than Angiosperms. Conifers are more evolutionarily advanced than other Gymnosperms, such as the ginkgos and cycads. They are more adapted to land conditions because their male sperms

Horse Chestnut seedling in July. The strap-like seed leaves are still attached to the seed case (conker) which will later drop off as the plant grows. In horse chestnuts, the seed leaves function as a food store while still in the seed and under the soil, and play no part in photosynthesis, unlike the seed leaves of many other tree species.

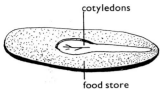

cotyledons

food store

Cross-section of an ungerminated ash seed showing the embryo plant in its food store of endoderm cells. The cotyledons, which are centrally placed at the bulbous end of the embryo, absorb the food material before they emerge above the ground.

are pollen dust, which can be wind blown to effect pollination. All conifers are normally wind pollinated and some species produce vast quantities of pollen, much of which is wasted, but some falls between the scales of the female cones and makes contact with the ovules. In conifers, pollination consists of the transference of the pollen grains, not to a stigma, as in broadleaves, but directly to the part of the ovule called the nucellus.

Broadleaved trees

There are 300–400 families of Dicotyledon trees – ie broadleaves – in the world, and all the evidence points to tropical origins. Magnolias are the most primitive flowering trees living today, and their fossils have been found in rocks of the Jurassic period in Greenland, which at that time was much nearer to the Equator.

Today in the tropics broadleaved trees are evergreen, and do not shed all their leaves seasonally at once. Instead they shed them evenly in small quantities throughout the year. The deciduous or annual leaf-shedding habit probably evolved as trees, shrubs and herbs migrated north and south from the tropics to the temperate zones, where the seasons are more definite.

Dicotyledons include shrubs and herbs in addition to trees. The herbs have evolved the practice of growing, flowering and fruiting in spring and summer, then dying back in winter. The seeds lie dormant in the soil until the warmth of the following spring stimulates seed germination. This annual habit has also enabled herbs to flourish in the temperate zones, in response to the harsher winter conditions, and in soils unsuited for tree growth. Many botanists consider that trees were the precursors of the forest plants and that herbs evolved later, as a ground layer on the forest floor. In the process of development they have lost the woody quality of trees and shrubs, which was no longer necessary.

Broadleaved trees are not a natural group or genus in their own right, but contribute to many plant families. Some families do not contain trees, while others contain many trees or, in some cases, consist entirely of trees. The beech family, which includes oak, sweet chestnut and the elm, belongs to the latter category. Magnolias have no herb layer representatives, but the pea family, which includes the laburnums, judas trees and the false acacias, is represented by many herbs, including the vetches, trefoils and clovers.

Magnolia flowers have both the male and female parts contained within a calyx of sepals and a corolla of petals. Such bisexual flowers are known as 'perfect' flowers. In poplars, elms, oaks, birch and alders, the male and female flowers are

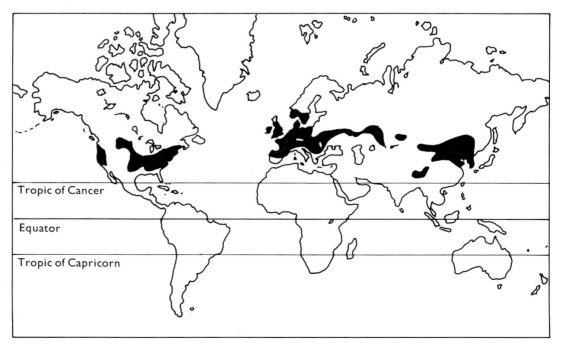

The main areas of broadleaved trees are in the temperate zones of the northern hemisphere. There are other forests in South America, Central Africa, Australia and New Zealand.

Tropic of Cancer

Equator

Tropic of Capricorn

separate and collected into catkins or tufts. Some flowers are without sepals or petals, and the sexes may be either on the same or different trees. In such trees, where the sexes are separate, the pollen is wind blown. In magnolias, limes, cherries, and horse chestnuts, where the sexes are in the same flower, the pollen is carried by insects. Wind-borne distribution evolved as an innovation at a later stage, possibly in response to the decreased diversity and abundance of insect life in temperate zones before the summer seasons began and the insects emerged in strength in their search for nectar.

The trunk and branches of both broadleaved and conifer trees are formed of bark, wood and pith, but the microscope reveals that the structure of the wood is different.

The leaves of broadleaves are thin, soft, flimsy and blade-like with a herring-bone pattern of veins. There are notable exceptions, such as the holly and the evergreen oaks which have leathery and spiny leaves. The typical shape of the broadleaved tree is narrowly or broadly domed, with the branches horizontal and spreading. In older trees there is a tendency for the lower branches to rest on the ground.

The branching habit and therefore the shape of a tree in its vigorous maturity is typical of a particular species, but a commonly occurring pattern of branching is

Magnolia flower opened to show sex organs

stigma · anthers · ovaries · tepals

Magnolia flowers are primitive, the 'tepals' not being differentiated into sepals and petals. Sepals in more evolutionarily advanced flowers form the calyx. The stamens are grooved along the length of the anthers, whereas in more advanced trees they are on the tips of the anthers. Many flowers have only one ovary or carpel while the magnolia has many, cladding the central cone of the flower.

discernible in trees as a whole, the ascending upper branches making a rounded or pointed top. The middle branches become progressively more down-sloped, the lowest branches often drooping or resting on the ground, because of their weight, especially in older trees.

Broadleaved woods are more important ecologically than conifer woods. They have a profusion of plant and insect life which is reflected in the numbers of birds which find sanctuary and food on the trees

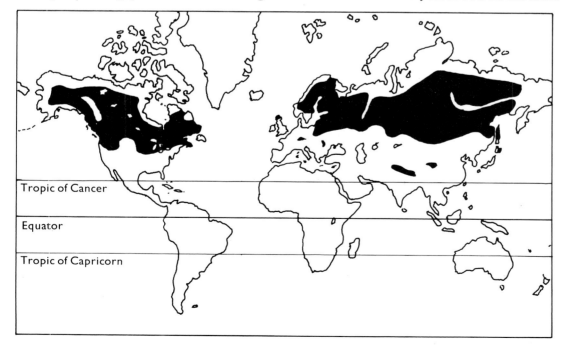

Tropic of Cancer · Equator · Tropic of Capricorn

The main distribution of coniferous forest in the world; there are pockets in mountainous areas elsewhere.

Key to Oak Tree Ecological Diagram

1. Rook
2. Woodcock
3. Kentish Glory
4. Jay
5. Tawny Owl
6. Wood Pigeon
7. Green Woodpecker
8. Nematode Worm
9. Centipede
10. Springtail
11. Earthworm
12. Ground Beetle larva
13. Nuthatch
14. Tree Creeper
15. Grey Squirrel
16. Purple Emperor
17. Marsh Tit
18. Wood Warbler

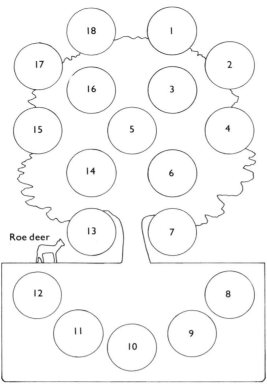

Roe deer

Key to Scots Pine Ecological Diagram

1. Long-eared Owl
2. Wood Warbler
3. Red Squirrel
4. Crossbill
5. Wild Cat
6. Pine Beetle (*Asemum striatum*)
7. Redworm
8. Millipede (*Proteroiulus fuscus*)
9. Centipede (*Lithoblus varigatus*)
10. Long Pine Weevil
11. Pine Marten
12. Capercaillie
13. Crested Tit
14. Goldcrest
15. Buzzard

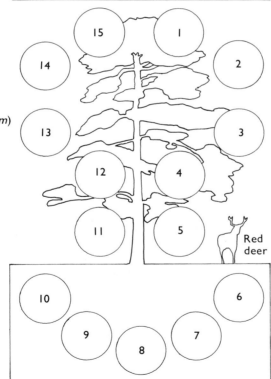

Red deer

or in the varied undergrowth. Many of Britain's most attractive birds are to be found in this type of woodland, including woodpeckers, jays, nuthatches, tits and bullfinches. This visual diversity is matched in broadleaved woodlands by the variety of birdsong – in particular that of warblers and that great virtuoso songster the nightingale.

Conifers

There is a distinct geographical division of conifers in the northern and another in the southern hemisphere. This probably originated long ago in the Earth's history when the land mass was divided into two supercontinents, separated by the ancient Tethys Sea, of which the Mediterranean, Black Sea, Dead Sea and Lake Baikal are surviving relics. For example, the monkey-puzzle trees, the yellow-woods of South America and Australasia, and the Tasmanian cedars of the redwood family are only native to the southern hemisphere. The remainder are located in the northern hemisphere, although there are exceptions, such as salients on high ground in the East Indies. Today, conifers are the dominant trees in the alpine, sub-arctic or boreal regions of the northern hemisphere.

Nearly all conifers are evergreen. There are some notable exceptions such as the larches and some species of redwoods, which shed their leaves in autumn in temperate zones. Conifer leaves are hard and needle-like or, in some groups, awl-like or scaly; they have a life of three to five years, and are shed continuously as the leaf litter under the trees testifies.

The conifer leaf shapes are adaptations against 'freeze drying' in sub-arctic winters, and the corresponding harsh conditions at higher altitudes nearer the equator. There appears to be a correlation between the length of the needles and the climate, with shorter needles on the species of the alpine and boreal regions, and longer ones on those of the sub-tropical and tropical regions. The needle-like form minimizes the area from which water can evaporate from within the leaf to the hot, or cold, dry atmosphere. Their outer surface is waxy and waterproof, and is provided with numerous openings or stomata. These stomata are able to open and close to allow the optimum amount of evaporation.

The shape typical of most conifers is a symmetrical, steep pyramid or spire, with a single straight trunk or bole extending to the top of the tree.

Conifers range in stature from the tallest trees in the world, the coast redwoods of California often exceeding 100m (328ft) in height, to the dwarf mountain pine *Pinus muga*, a native of the Pyrenees which sometimes does not exceed one metre (three feet three inches) in height. Even smaller are the prostrate common junipers of the sub-arctic regions, a mere few centimetres (an inch or so) high, but extending along the surface of the ground for a metre (just over three feet) or so.

Numerous cultivars and dwarf forms have been developed from conifers and are very common in parks and gardens throughout Britain. The ability of Lawson's Cypress naturally to produce mutants has enabled cultivators to produce in excess of 200 varieties.

Many fast-growing conifers are planted commercially because of their ability to grow on poor soils. On the acid soils of moorland and mountainous terrain, and on some marginal lowlands in Britain, exotic conifers have been planted extensively. This practice is causing considerable concern to conservationists, because such planting means the destruction of many habitats of uncommon birds.

Remains of the Lepidodendron family in the fossil grove at Victoria Park, Glasgow. These trees existed at the same time as the forests which were responsible for the coal measures of central Scotland. (*Crown copyright reserved*)

2: THE ANCESTRY OF TREES

In response to the dramatic and radical changes our planet has undergone since the beginning of geological times – the movements of the continents, their separations and collisions, the elevation of the mountain ranges and the climatic variations in the various regions of the world – markedly different forest types have developed. Those plants and animals which have been unable to adapt to the changes have become extinct, like the giant horsetails and the dinosaurs.

The earliest land plants

Although there is no conclusive evidence in the form of fossils, it is reasonable to infer that land plants evolved from marine algae. These algae contained amino acids and chlorophyll, the necessary ingredients for an initial transition to living terrestrial plants.

In 1913 geologist Dr W Mackie discovered fossils showing with perfect clarity plant remains of the Early Devonian period in deposits of chert (silica) at Rhynie, Aberdeenshire. Four different plants were identified and have been named *Rhynie A*, *R major*, *R horneophyton* and *R asteroxylon*. Although these plants contained the necessary requirements for life on land, they had not severed their marine connections.

The fossil record of conifers can be traced back to the Carboniferous age (300,000,000 years ago). Although the primitive species living at that time became extinct, all the surviving species are ancient in origin. The very distinctive Monkey-puzzle tree and the redwoods extend back to the beginning of the Jurassic period, and the pine family has been in existence since Early Cretaceous times (135,000,000 years ago).

During the Triassic, Jurassic and Cretaceous periods trees steadily evolved and those which were better adapted to life on land, the conifers, supplanted the other Gymnosperm ancestral trees although one, the Maidenhair Tree, *Ginkgo biloba*, still survives in gardens and parks today. By the Cretaceous period the

Angiosperm flowering trees were established and were exerting their dominance over the conifers.

Fossil evidence from this period shows the existence of the Dawn Redwood, *Metasequoia glyptostroboides*, which was considered to be an extinct species until rediscovered in China in 1941. It was brought to England in 1948 and is now to be seen in many gardens and parks.

Trees in Britain in the Tertiary era

In the early part of the Eocene period, south-east England bordered on the edge of a land mass embracing a vast tropical freshwater lake. Nypa palms and other tropical vegetation had colonized the land closest to the water's edge, hippopotamus abounded in the water, and magnolias grew on the higher ground. The scene showed some similarities to the coastal vegetation of the East Indies and New Guinea today.

During the course of the Tertiary era, which lasted from the Palaeocene period until the end of the Pliocene period, and preceded the glaciations, the tree vegetation became progressively less tropical. In Pliocene times the trees of Europe and Britain were composed of the thermophilous or warmth-demanding species of semi-tropical and warm temperate climates. These included the Japanese Umbrella Pine, the Swamp Cypress, the Magnolia, the Tulip Tree, the Sweet Gum, and the Red and Scarlet Oaks.

Conifers, including hemlocks and thujas (Western Red and White Cedars), were also present at higher altitudes. These trees may be seen today growing wild at similar altitudes in North America, China and Japan. At the same time, the English Oak, elms, ash, hornbeam and limes were consolidating their presence. Such an assemblage of diverse species is probably without parallel.

The glaciations

In Europe, the warmth-loving trees of the Tertiary era were progressively killed off by the successive glaciations of the Pleistocene period, which began about two million years ago.

The diversity of tree species in North America, China and Japan greatly exceeds that of Europe, yet the glaciations experienced by those countries were as severe as the European glaciations. The reason for this phenomenon is that in America, for example, the mountain ranges run north-south. This allowed the warmth-loving trees to retreat through valleys between the mountains to warmer refuges in the south, before the advance of the ice-sheets and tundra. The trees returned by the same route to recolonize the land as the ice-sheets retreated. In Europe, by contrast, the mountain ranges extend from west to east, from the Pyrenees to the Tatra mountains in Romania.

Furthermore, there is a high plateau between the Pyrenees and the Alps. Hence, retreat to the warmer refuges in the south was cut off for the thermophilous trees and so they perished, never to return until reintroduced in recent times. Many of these trees are now thriving, mainly up to the latitude of southern England, and in sheltered areas further north. There were four glaciations, interspersed with three warm inter-glacial periods, when the vegetation returned in the wake of the retreating ice-sheets. Each successive glaciation killed off more trees until Europe was left with the relatively impoverished assemblage of tree species it has today.

The first or pre-Cromerian glaciation was relatively mild and did not reach further south than the Midlands. The second, the Lowestoft Glaciation, was

LEFT:
Artist's impression of the Carboniferous period. During this time Britain lay in the sub-tropical and tropical latitudes, and the climate allowed the growth of luxuriant forests.

1. Lepidodendrons, a club-moss
2. Calamites, a horsetail
3. Sigallaria
4. A fern

OVERLEAF, LEFT:
A geological time scale with a brief summary of the evolution of land plants

OVERLEAF, RIGHT:
Flandrian Chart – a schematic representation of the history of forest cover in Britain since the retreat of the ice-sheets. Adapted from *The History of British Flora* by Sir Harry Godwin.

ERAS	PERIODS	EPOCHS	AGE IN MILLION YEARS BC	MAJOR DEVELOPMENTS OF PLANT LIFE AS SHOWN IN THE FOSSIL RECORD	CLIMATIC & OROGENIC EVENTS	MILESTONES OF ANIMAL LIFE
CENOZOIC	Quaternary	Recent (Holocene)	0–1	Recolonization by surviving tree flora of Europe, later affected by forest clearance, as elsewhere in the world.	Temperate in Europe	
		Pleistocene	1–2	At least four successive glaciations destroy the surviving Tertiary tree species in Europe. In the temperate inter-glacial periods, the forests returned.	The glaciations	
	Tertiary	Pliocene	2–5	Cooling of climate reduces thermophilous trees in Europe. Temperate climate forest trees dominate, eg oak, elm. More definite zoning of world tree-cover.	Zoning of cooling world climates	
		Miocene	5–25	Temporary regional forest recession. Herbs increase.	Mountain building	
		Oligocene	25–38	Extension of 'modern' forests giving almost complete forest cover with great diversity of species, eg oaks, limes, elms, magnolias, sweet gums, redwoods, wingnuts. Decline of tropical elements of tree-cover in Europe.	Warm, temperate	
		Eocene	38–55	Tropical rain forest and Malaysian-type vegetation, with diversity of palms, including Nypa, prevailing on the lowlands of Britain; magnolias in abundance on high ground.	Warm to hot worldwide	
		Palaeocene	55–65	Almost complete domination of the flora by Angiosperms (flowering plants), mainly trees. Conifers retreat to high ground.		Explosion of mammal population
MESOZOIC	Upper Cretaceous		65–135	Tree-size Angiosperms begin to dominate the forests eg magnolias, figs, oaks and maples. Proliferation of Angiosperms eg magnolias widespread.	Fluctuating world climates, generally warm and equable	Demise of dinosaurs
	Lower Cretaceous		135–150	Early Gymnosperms decline, particularly cycads; ginkgos and advanced conifers, including redwoods, still dominate the vegetation.		
	Jurassic		150–190	Earliest known Angiosperms (flowering plants). Cycads, ginkgos and conifers dominate the vegetation. Primitive Gymnosperms disappear.		First mammals Dinosaurs dominant
	Triassic		190–230	Proliferation of cycads and conifers, some conifers resembling Monkey-puzzle tree *(Araucaria)*. Cycads dominant vegetation. Disappearance of seed ferns.		Early dinosaurs
PALAEOZOIC	Permian		230–280	Reduction of tree-sized club mosses, and horsetails, which became herbs. Early Gymnosperms, eg cycads, including *Glossopteris* (a seed fern), ginkgos and early conifers.	Glaciations and widespread aridity	Early reptiles
	Upper Carboniferous		280–325	Vast, humid lowland forests of tree-sized club-mosses, horsetails, tree and seed ferns, and early Gymnosperms, eg Cordatailes, protoconifers. Their remains formed the coal measures.	No polar ice caps; hot and humid worldwide	Age of amphibians
	Lower Carboniferous		325–350	Further proliferation of early ferns, eg *Staurplexus*. Early tree-sized horsetails, eg *Calamites*, and club-mosses eg *Lepidodendron*.		
	Devonian		350–395	Psilopsids flourished and declined. *Rhynia major* is an important Psilopsid fossil from the Rhynie Chert beds, Aberdeenshire. Tree-sized forests of early club-mosses, and Gymnosperms flourished, the latter the first to increase girth by cambium growth. The first photo-synthesizing leaves evolved.	Mild and equable worldwide	
	Silurian		395–440	*Cooksonia* and *Steganothecus striata* from deposits in USSR are the first known vascular land plants. They had simple, leafless, multi-forked stems, little differentiated from the roots. They belonged to the Psilopsids, ancestral to all land plants.		

AGE BEFORE PRESENT	DOMINANT TREES IN FORESTS AT ANY GIVEN TIME, AND OTHER VEGETATION	EXTENT OF FOREST COVER	CLIMATIC PERIODS	CLIMATIC AND CULTURAL EFFECTS ON THE FORESTS. GEOLOGICAL, CULTURAL AND OTHER EVENTS	CULTURES	
	Reafforestation. Introduction of alien trees. Tree-cover, in the form of semi-natural woods, spinneys, plantations, coppices and hedgerows. Yew woods on southern calcareous hills. Proliferation of beech in south east, etc. Clearing of closed forest which favoured ash, hornbeam and beech. Return of birch as colonizing tree.	Urbanization Arable land Pasture Rough land	SUB-ATLANTIC Cool and wet	Nearly all 'wild' forest cleared by Tudor times. Progressive clearing of forest between expanding villages and towns. Clearing of lowland clay valleys and plains begins. Celtic farming. Deteriorating climate overwhelms log causeways on Somerset Levels.	NORMANS JUTES ANGLES SAXONS ROMANS IRON AGE BRONZE AGE	FLANDRIAN POST-GLACIAL PERIOD
2000 —						
	Semi-natural forest dominated by oak and ash, with birch. Oak and elm dominant in calcareous regions. Ash increases as clearing of closed forest progresses.		SUB-BOREAL Warmer and drier than today	Forest clearing on Dartmoor and calcareous Downs. Bogs dry out. Breckland deforestation begins. Forest grazing and shifting settlements begin to change the forests and open up pastures.	NEOLITHIC	
4000 —	Lime decreases. Dramatic decrease in elm due to selective exploitation.	FOREST CLEARING BEGINS		ELM DECLINE		
	Closed forests dominated by oak, lime and elm, each species dominant in its favoured regions. Lime trees spread but do not reach Ireland. Closed forest displaces birch south of the highlands. Spread of alder as damp situations expand. Treeless terrain, coastal and montane.	Climax forest PRIMARY FOREST	ATLANTIC Climax of warmth and wetness	Arrival of cattle-grazing invaders. CLIMATIC OPTIMUM (almost complete forest cover) Expansion of raised and blanket bogs. Birch forests overwhelmed in Pennines, Wales, Cumbria and Scotland. Pines smothered in Scotland and Ireland. BRITAIN BECOMES AN ISLAND	MESOLITHIC	
6000 —						
8000 —	Arrival of oak, elm, and alder as forest trees. Lime, a late arrival. Pine forests dominant, giving way to broadleaves in south. Hazel forms pure woods and under-storey for pines.		BOREAL Warm and dry	Sea-level rising. Small population of nomadic hunters and nut gatherers, exerting no impact on the forest. Mires dry out, some becoming tree clad eg with pines in the East Anglian fens.		
10,000 —	Birch forest, rowan, aspen, and juniper. Pine abundant in the south.	Raw soil	PRE-BOREAL Sub-arctic; milder	North Sea still dry. (Sea-level 92–122 metres or 3–400 feet lower than today).		
	Dwarf birch and willow. Juniper. Alpine plants eg Dryas.	Grass-sedge and open	UPPER DRYAS Arctic cold	Return of corrie glaciers to Cumbria and North Wales.		
	Birch, aspen, rowan and willows, solitary and forming woods and copses. Juniper.		ALLEROD INTER-STADIAL Milder	Park tundra. Some woodland.	UPPER PALAEOLITHIC	LATE WEICHSELIAN GLACIATION
12,000 —	Dwarf birch and willow. Juniper, heather, crowberry and alpine herbs, including Mountain Aven (Dryas octopetal).	herbaceous tundra vegetation	LOWER DRYAS Arctic cold	Permafrost in south. Slumping of thawed soil on Bodmin Moor.	NB The Flandian Chart time scale is based upon years before the present day, not at the more usual AD/BC	

much more severe, with ice-sheets to a depth of 800-900m (875–984yds). It advanced southwards to just north of the River Thames. The third, the Gipping Glaciation, extended from the Welsh mountains down to the River Severn and eastwards to a line just above the most southerly point of the Lowestoft Glaciation. The last glaciation is called the Weichselian, or the New Drift, and during this period Ireland was connected to Britain.

Interspersed between these major glaciations were relatively mild interludes when the extreme cold relented, and the broadleaved forests returned.

Pollen analysis

The application of new techniques of pollen analysis has led to great advances in the study of prehistoric vegetation. It is particularly revealing when used on deposits laid down since the last glaciation. By extracting sections of silt from lakes, or peat from fens or bogs, it is possible to examine layers in their successive sequence for their pollen content. A device like a soil borer cylinder is used for this purpose. Tree pollen is very light and may be carried many miles by the wind. The outer casing of the pollen grains is almost indestructible in the conditions of natural decay that occur in peat bogs. By examining the pollen grains in the layers of these cores, it is possible to correlate the sequence of changes that have occurred in Britain since the last Ice Age. The types of pollen grain present in a particular layer give an indication of the climatic condition existing at the time of deposition. The ratio of tree and herbaceous plant pollen is an indicator of the relationship between woodland and more open terrain.

The Pre-Boreal period

With the remission of the final major glaciation about 10,000 years ago, the Pleistocene period came to an end, to be succeeded by the Holocene, or Recent period, in which we live today. As the temperature improved trees increased and replaced the open glacial vegetation. The last 12,000 years have seen a number of climatic fluctuations which, though minor in comparison with those associated with the great glaciations, have nonetheless had a significant impact upon Britain's vegetation.

The first of these fluctuations is known as the Pre-Boreal period, and lasted from about 8000 to 7500 BC. The sub-arctic climate of the end of the Pleistocene persisted, but the summers were warmer, allowing birch to return in profusion and to form forests. Willows invaded the wetter areas, while Hazel and Alder, Oaks and Elms made their first post-glacial appearance. Due to the huge amount of water still locked in the ice-sheets, the sea-level was about ninety metres (295ft) lower than today's levels. This resulted in the emergence of an uninterrupted land-bridge between Britain and the Continent which allowed the migration of tree species to Britain and Ireland.

For example, the Strawberry Tree, *Arbutus unedo*, spread from the Mediterranean regions to become established along the now submerged coast, to Ireland, where it is locally abundant in the extreme south west. Pollen grains of birch and mosses have been dredged from the North Sea, confirming that the land submerged between the east coast of Britain and the lowland of Belgium and Holland was previously a plain of Birch woodland, probably with Alder present as well.

The Boreal period

This period lasted from about 7500 to 5500 BC; during it the climate became warmer and drier than it is today – decidedly Mediterranean in character. Hazel became a very important tree, forming the under-storey vegetation for the advancing pine forests. Broadleaved trees including the Elm, the Lime and the Oak superseded the pines over much of Britain. In the south of England oak became the dominant tree, a condition that persists today. Birch was prominent in the north and west. During the latter part of this period there was a continual interchange of tree species on a local basis, except in those locations where pines had consolidated their position on the poorer soils.

The Atlantic period

The Atlantic period succeeded the Boreal period, and lasted from about 5500 to 3500 BC. The climate was wetter, but remained warm – ideal conditions for the proliferation of the oak forests. Alder increased its range from the lower valleys to the higher ground and merged with the oaks.

The forests spread up the flanks of the mountains, reaching the 1000m (3280ft) contour. Wych Elm and limes were common, and Hazel was the dominant under-storey shrub. Scots Pines dominated the Scottish Highlands and oaks spread farther north into the glens.

Sphagnum moss invaded the fens and formed raised bogs. The trees retreated from the water-logged ground, while the water reached higher levels on the elevated plateaux, so destroying established birch and pine forests.

The Sub-Boreal period

During the Atlantic period, the Mesolithic hunter-gatherers had already fashioned flints for many domestic purposes. However, they had little or no impact on the forests. During the latter stages of the Atlantic period, the first waves of Neolithic settlers and farmers arrived from the Continent with their polished stone axes, seeds and beasts. Their axes were very efficient tree-felling implements, as recent experiments have proved. Burning also had an important role to play in the creation of pasture-land. Initially, the land they cleared was on the higher ground and drier areas.

During the Bronze Age, about 4000 years ago, these people utilized the existing metals, especially copper and tin, for making domestic utensils and agricultural tools. This development enabled them to cultivate upland areas; Dartmoor was deforested and the chalk downlands were almost totally cleared of trees at this time.

The Sub-Atlantic period

At the beginning of the Sub-Atlantic period, 2500 years before the present day, climatic conditions deteriorated from the warm and dry of the Sub-Boreal period to cold and wet – in essence the climate we have today. There have been warm and cold variations since, but not of sufficient duration or extremity to have had a significant effect on the vegetation. The arrival of a cold and wet climate allowed the development of raised and blanket bogs in areas which had previously been

dry heaths. These sphagnum peat bogs preserved pollen grains in their layers of deposition and thus play an important role in the accuracy of vegetation dating and distribution. The climatic change also favoured birch, and considerable re-colonization of this species occurred. Beech spread in southern England together with some increase in hornbeam and alder.

The spread of the Iron Age arrived from the eastern Mediterranean countries and, as iron was widely distributed throughout Britain, it soon superseded bronze for the making of tools. The iron-bladed plough allowed the cultivation of lowland clay areas, which caused some loss of oaks.

The Belgic invaders, themselves Celts, arrived about 2100 years ago, introducing further improved agricultural techniques, including the wheeled plough. This innovation enabled them to cultivate the loamy soils of East Anglia, Essex, Hampshire, the Thames Valley and the coastal plains of Kent and Sussex after the trees had been felled. Their methods proved so successful they were able to export their surplus grain to the Continent.

The Roman occupation

By the time of the Roman invasion, the great forests of the Weald and the Midland plains still remained. The Romans were mainly concerned with road engineering and the development of cities, which had a limited effect on the forests. However, they were also sophisticated agriculturalists, and their farming system, based on villa estates, was widely adopted throughout Britain, particularly in the south and west, until the fourth century AD (1600 years ago). What effect it had on the forest cover is hard to assess, but the Romans introduced many trees, including Medlar Thorn and Horse Chestnut, the latter now established as a wild tree.

Anglo-Saxon settlers

After the Romans abandoned Britain shortly after AD 400 (1600 years ago), the country underwent a period of gradual settlement by the Angles and Saxons from Germany and the Jutes from Denmark. Over a period of time they adopted a more intensive agricultural policy than their predecessors and made drastic inroads into the primary forests on the clay soils of lowland Britain. Initially they displaced the Celtic peoples from their farms on the fertile loams of the coastal regions of Kent. Further incursions into the farmland continued together with destruction of the forests.

As they spread, they established village communities, a process which continued until the Celtic peoples had been driven to their final refuges in Cornwall and Wales. The abandoned Celtic field systems on the downlands which did not revert to woodland and scrub became grazing for vast flocks of sheep. The Vikings supplanted the Saxons in the northern regions of England and settled on already cultivated land. Their arrival did not cause any further significant changes to the tree cover.

The Norman conquest

By the time of the Norman conquest in 1066, the extensive tracts of forest which had covered most of Britain in former times were no more. The forest remained only on the less fertile soils and the more inaccessible areas of the country. These remaining forests were very important to the Saxon hunters.

After the conquest was complete, the Normans began their suppression of the Saxons by intimidation, looting and destruction of their farms. Bands of Saxons retreated to the remaining forests and fens, where they lived as outlaws. The Normans consolidated their conquest through the rigorous application of the feudal system and a high degree of centralized organization. Under the direction of successive kings and their barons, they exploited the land's resources. During the next two centuries, despite interminable disputes between the kings and the barons, the peasants tilled their plots to maintain a meagre diet, sometimes supplemented by food obtained from the forests, often illegally.

Cattle grazing too had a dramatic effect on the forests. The browsing and trampling destroyed the developing seedlings of oaks and other trees, preventing regeneration. However, pigs were not so detrimental to the forests, as they destroyed many of the pests that ate the tree seeds and seedlings. Unpalatable thorns were ignored by the cattle and so thorny scrubland developed along the fringes of the forests. This type of common land exists today in localized areas in northern England and may be a relic from this period.

The forest laws William the Conqueror created the Royal Forests, including the New Forest, the Forest of Dean and the Peak Forest. The total area of land annexed by the sovereign amounted to approximately one-third of England. The Royal Forests in a legal sense covered not only the forests, but also the towns, villages and farms within their boundaries. At the beginning of this new regime, barbaric penalties were exacted by the overlords for the killing of wildlife. Even the taking of wood for their fires and the building and repair of their homes was forbidden in the Royal Forests. Regardless of the punitive effects of the new laws, the people very largely ignored them. However, these laws resulted in large areas of the forests being preserved.

The Later Middle Ages

With the relaxation of forest laws an intensive agricultural regime advanced again. Further clearing of the forests occurred, and cattle were allowed to graze freely within them. Hence regeneration was at a minimum. There was an increase of thorny scrubland as old trees died, or were felled for the repair of buildings.

Although some forest survived, the landscape of Britain, apart from the mountainous areas of Wales, Scotland and northern England, was now mainly pastoral and agricultural. The Cistercian monks were probably the most efficient farmers of the twelfth century. They perfected estate management, and thereby contributed greatly to the country's economy, especially through their development of the wool trade. But they were also responsible for the felling of trees on a large scale.

By the fourteenth century, the estimated population of sheep was over 8,000,000 compared with a human population of 2,000,000. These figures are an indication of the vast area of grassland during this period. The ratio of pasture to arable land depended upon the fluctuating prices of wool and corn.

From Tudor times to the present day

Throughout the Tudor period there was continued felling of native oaks for the construction of ships. By the latter part of the seventeenth century Samuel Pepys, naval administrator to Charles II, arranged for the importation of oak from the Continent, because England's native oak was no longer adequate for the needs of the shipbuilders. However, the main cause for the depletion of forest during this period was the use of wood for iron-smelting and other industries requiring large quantities of fuel. To meet this demand coppicing of oak and hazel increased, a method known as coppice-with-standards, and it is still practised locally today; a good example can be seen in Ham Street Woods National Nature Reserve in Kent.

Until the eighteenth century some pasture still remained open for the grazing of cattle, sheep, deer and horses. But between 1760 and 1800, the Enclosure Acts reduced the open field system to a walled and hedgerow agriculture, the result being the people were denied their rights of pasture and faggot gathering from the woodlands. The enclosures had become necessary, however, because of the rising population and the need for increased crop production.

In Scotland the situation was even more desperate, as the valleys and glens which contained many virgin forests were being ruthlessly destroyed for charcoal to fire the bloomeries throughout Scotland, for the manufacture of cannons. There was also a considerable increase in sheep farming in the Lowlands, the consequence being further felling and burning of trees, and so today we are left with a few remnants of those once great oak and pine forests. Many Scottish landowners made great efforts to halt this depletion of trees by planting mainly Scots Pine. Foremost among these early conservationists was Sir Alexander Grant, who planted the native pine by the million.

The need for timber during World War I became so desperate, especially towards the end, that the Government realized the paucity of home-grown timber and, in 1919, the Forestry Commission was established. Mainly exotic conifers were planted, but with some Scots Pine, on existing woodland sites, heaths and moorlands. During World War II, with the great need for increased food production, 'permanent' grass was ploughed up and some adjacent woodlands were felled to facilitate cultivation.

From 1950 onwards there has been large scale 'grubbing up' of hedgerows, reducing many hedgerow trees, especially oaks, elms and hawthorns. Recently, however, there has been a reversal of this policy due to loss of topsoil, and some hedgerows have been planted.

Plant hunters and the introduction of new trees

Considerable credit has been given to the intrepid plant hunters of the seventeenth to twentieth centuries, and justly so. What must not be forgotten is our indebtedness, as a nation, to the sponsors of those adventurers, and to the skills of the lanscape designers of these centuries. Today, their foresight, courage and conviction allows millions of visitors to view, in tranquil settings, the fulfilment of their labours – a fulfilment which they themselves could never have expected to see in their own lifetimes.

Although many tree introductions were made from Roman times onwards, for food and medicinal purposes, it was in the reign of Charles I that the first recorded organized overseas plant expedition took place. This was the visit of John Tradescant Senior to Holland on behalf of Lord Salisbury to collect plants for his estate. His acquisitions included many fruit trees, as well as limes and sycamores.

John Tradescant the Younger (1608–62) decided upon the New World as his source of plants to be introduced to Britain. The trees and other plants he sent to his father in Lambeth greatly enhanced the gardens and parks of their benefactors. Included in his collection was that most graceful of plants, the Tulip Tree.

The Tradescant name will always be associated with the London Plane, *Platanus X hispanica*. The younger Tradescant sent seeds of *Platanus occidentalis* to his father at his London home in Lambeth, where *Platanus orientalis* was already established. In due course the two crossed and the result was London's ubiquitous tree, the London Plane.

Although not a plant hunter, the name of Sir John Evelyn is honoured by many concerned with the conservation of trees. He was born at Wooton, near Dorking, Surrey in 1620 and died there in 1706. His diaries are almost as famous as those of his great friend Samuel Pepys. He was commissioned by Charles II, after the Restoration, to undertake an investigation into the depletion of trees suitable for the construction of ships. The result was *Sylva*, a book which describes the cultivation of the most important trees for timber production. Four editions were published, each being modified and enlarged, to include information on soils and herbaceous plants. After his death further editions were published by various authors, the last in 1825. His writing was influential and encouraged the planting of trees, largely on country estates.

David Douglas (1779–1834) was born in Perthshire and, at the age of ten, was apprenticed as a gardener to Lord Mansfield. When he was twenty-one he joined the staff of the Royal Botanic Gardens in Glasgow. Due to his enthusiasm and dedication to his work, he was invited to discover and collect plants in North America. One of his first discoveries was the tree that bears his name, the Douglas Fir, *Pseudotsuga menziesii*. It was introduced into Britain in about 1827. In addition to the many lupins, mahonias and clarkias, he discovered the Western Red Cedar, and his notes contained descriptions of the giant sequoias. His death occurred quite tragically on the Island of Hawaii, where he was undertaking further searches for new botanical specimens.

George Forrest (1873–1932) became attracted to travel when he visited relatives in Australia and he visited South Africa on his return to Scotland. He started his working life in a chemist's shop, and the turning point of his career was an offer of work at the Royal Botanical Gardens in Edinburgh. In 1903 he was offered the opportunity to collect plants in China, which he readily accepted. In the river valleys he discovered many rhododendrons, camellias, magnolias and orchids. His collections also included maples and various conifers.

A further debt as a nation is owed to those imaginative people who were responsible for the establishment of gardens and parks where the exotic plants collected by the plant hunters can be seen, in particular, the two Royal Botanic Gardens at Kew and Edinburgh, and the National Trust. The latter was established in 1895 and is responsible for more than 240,642 hectares (600,000 acres), which includes over one hundred gardens and in addition to the gardens, amongst its priceless treasures are the mountainsides of Snowdonia, the Lake District and the Derbyshire Peak District.

3: NATIVE TREES

The criterion for applying the term native to a tree in Britain, is that authoritative proof exists of the tree's existence on British soil before the separation from Continental Europe, about 7500 years ago. At this period the rising sea-level was gradually inundating the last land bridge, creating the British Isles of today.

The evidence for native trees is based upon the rare fossil or mineral fragments available, and the analysis of pollen samples taken from lake deposits or peat bogs. There are thirty-three or thirty-four native trees known to have been in existence at the time of the separation. However, it is possible that other trees existed for which pollen predating early Atlantic times has not yet been found or identified. Other trees may have arrived by natural processes and not by deliberate introduction, perhaps contained in seed for crops or carried here by birds.

Perhaps the status of native should be granted to those warmth-loving trees which were natives before elimination by the glaciations. These would include the sweet gums, tupelos, tulip trees and other magnolias, the red and scarlet oaks, and others. If, after reintroduction in recent times, they have proved to be hardy, it seems unjust to deny them the native status which would add to the richness of the catalogue of our native tree flora.

Hybridization

Natural hybridization between tree species within the same genus is an evolutionary process that has been constantly occurring throughout the ages, since plants first evolved, and it continues today. Consequently, the identification of some species of native trees in many localities in Britain requires caution. For example, English Oak, *Quercus robur*, and Sessile Oak, *Quercus petraea*, have been hybridizing wherever their preferential habitats overlap. In certain localities in Sherwood Forest the majority of oaks are hybrids. In the Sevenoaks area of Kent, a recent survey found that all field oaks investigated were hybrids, with more characteristics of the Sessile than the English Oak. On the North Downs of Surrey and Kent both species occur, but there are many hybrids and some woods contain only hybrids.

It does appear that native oaks as a pure species are being hybridized out of existence. However, conclusive identification is possible of the English Oak in the natural oak-woods of ancient commons on clay belts of the Surrey and Sussex Weald, where they are some distance from Sessile Oaks. Conversely, in Sessile Oak country of the hilly districts of western and northern Britain, the purity of the species is still intact.

Turkey Oak, *Quercus cerris*, has been planted in some woods and has readily hybridized with the native English Oak, which in some localities may account for the suspiciously narrow leaves of many wild oaks encountered.

Similar uncertainty is encountered when attempting to identify elms in the field. Most are hybrids, of two or more parent species, or even hybrids crossed with introduced elms. Already, some pure native species may have been hybridized out of existence.

Most elms seen in the field in southern England are not identifiable, defying even the skills of the experts. Many are hybrids between Wych Elm, *Ulmus glabra*, and Small-leafed Elm, *Ulmus carpinifolia*, both native trees. The English Elm, *Ulmus procera*, despite its name, may be a hybrid of parent species that flourished on land now beneath the English Channel. The present distribution range confirms this theory. It is a common tree in northwest France and was common in southern England and East Anglia, before Dutch Elm Disease struck in 1970.

Where the English Elm is at the extreme of its northern range it reproduces by suckers. Hence in these areas it is a clone, only reproducing vegetatively: not being able to hybridize with other species, it maintains its specific purity.

There are two models of classification of elms today. One does not recognize either the Plot Elm, *Ulmus plotii*, or the Coritanian Elm, *Ulmus coritana*, and designates the Cornish Elm as a variety of the Smooth-leafed Elm.

Care must also be exercised when identifying two native birches, the Silver Birch, *Betula pendula*, and the White Birch, *Betula pubescens*. They thrive in similar habitats, though the latter needs slightly more moisture, and they hybridize very easily.

NATIVE TREES

Woodlands are a cherished feature of Britain's landscape, as well as important reservoirs of wildlife. Certain types of woodland are more important than others, the most valuable being the semi-natural woodland made up of native tree species, such as oak, beech, birch, alder and ash. These may be direct fragments – albeit modified – of Britain's primitive natural forests.

Trees known to have been present in Britain, before it was isolated from Continental Europe about 7500 years ago, are considered to be the true native species. There are definitely thirty-three species, and if five shrubby willows and three controversial elms are included, the number is forty-one. As previously stated they are difficult to identify with confidence and also may have been the result of introduction in late prehistoric times. The native tree descriptions that follow are in the order in which the trees appeared in Britain.

Common Yew
Taxus baccata
Yews are evergreen trees and are among the most impressive and characteristic of the southern chalk downlands, and are found frequently in limestone areas elsewhere in Britain. They are popular in parks and gardens where they are often used for topiary, and in churchyards where there are specimens estimated to be over 1000 years old. There is considerable variation in height, from ten to twenty-five metres (thirty-three to eighty-two feet).

The Kingley Vale National Nature Reserve near Chichester contains one of the finest yew woods remaining in Europe. Although many of the gnarled and deeply fissured trees look very ancient, they are probably very little over 500 years old. The wood is extremely hard and slow-growing and the bark is smooth and reddish-brown to purple in colour. It peels continuously in strips and this gives the trunk its patchy appearance. The trunk and branches are often covered with sprouting foliage.

The crown is variable, conic in some trees and broadly domed in others, especially in multi-boled trees. The lower branches of old trees often rest on the ground and from these new trees occasionally grow, the rampant new shoots giving trees a ragged outline. Frequently yew trees join together to make one tree and only close examination will determine this fact. This adds to the difficulties in determining the age of the Yew.

The leaves are strap-like and set spirally on the shoots, very dark green and shiny above, dull yellow-green below. The trees are either male or female, the male flowers being small globular vessels clustered on the underside of last year's shoots. They turn yellowish from February to March and shed copious clouds of pollen. The female flowers have minute green embryo berries and when they are ripe they swell into a fleshy translucent aril or red pulp which is sweet and edible – an important food source for many birds and mammals. The black seed, which is poisonous, is embedded within it with its top exposed.

Common Juniper
Juniperus communis
A widespread plant of the temperate and sub-arctic regions, the Common Juniper is a native on the southern downlands, northern limestone areas and the Scottish highlands. In early post-glacial times it was abundant throughout the country. It was the first tree to colonize the soil deposited after the retreat of the ice-sheets some 10,000 years ago. Now it is much less common than formerly; on the South Downs, for example, it has been suppressed by the yews and other longer living trees, for which it served as nursery cover.

The shape varies from an erect, slender tree or bush to a prostrate mat-like shrub on the more exposed northern mountains.

A lifespan of 200 years is known, though this is exceptional. In young trees, rigid branches grow vertically upwards to produce a dense, spire-shaped crown, but this shape is often affected by the elements, resulting in more ragged, less formal-looking tops. They make bushes or trees, rarely exceeding three metres (ten feet) in height in the open, but can grow to ten metres (thirty-three feet) in sheltered situations. Growth is no more than a few centimetres a year. More than one bole or stem is common. The reddish-brown bark is stringy and peels away in flakes.

The leaves are sharp needles in whorls of three, light green-grey and about one centimetre (about half an inch) in length. The Juniper is wind-pollinated, and the male and female 'flowers' are on separate trees. The males, which bear the pollen sacs, are minute, yellowish-white, solitary cones of granular appearance. The female 'flowers' are cups of three to eight green scales clustered under the twigs. After pollination they expand and cover the single seed by autumn to form a hard green 'berry', which eventually becomes fleshy and bluish-black in colour with a

ABOVE:
Common Juniper
Juniperus communis

LEFT:
Common Yew *Taxus baccata*

33

bloom. They are tempting to birds, which disperse them via their digestive systems.

Scots Pine
Pinus sylvestris

The Scots Pine is the only native cone-bearing tree, and, with the Yew and Common Juniper, one of only three native Gymnosperms. It was an early pioneer from glacial times. Once, until some 8000 years ago, the Scots Pine covered vast areas of Britain, before it was superseded by broadleaved trees in England and Wales. Still surviving are remnants of the original native pine forests in the Scottish Highlands: notable fragments remain on Deeside, the Cairngorms, Rannoch Moor and in Wester Ross. In 1660 it was reintroduced to southern England as a planted tree and has since been widely used for

landscaping and as a commercial tree. It has been widely planted in the south and west of Britain, mainly on the acid heathland where it has become naturalized and has re-established itself as a wild tree. In recent years it has been superseded as a commercial tree by faster growing introduced conifers such as the Corsican Pine and the Sitka Spruce.

Initially, in isolated trees, the crown is conical. In older trees it tends to spread and become flat-topped or even billowy on a long branchless bole, occasionally reaching a height of forty to fifty metres (130–165ft). In dense plantations these shapes are somewhat suppressed. The tree may live for up to 400 years or more.

The bark of a mature tree is dark reddish-brown and fissured into elongated plates. It is tinged with yellow

Scots Pine *Pinus sylvestris*

or pink towards the top. Towards the crown it becomes smoother and a deeper red. The blue-green needles are five to seven centimetres (two to three and a quarter inches) long, and are set in scaly sheaths in pairs, often with a spiral twist.

The small male cones are usually yellow, though sometimes crimson, and are densely clustered round the lower portions of the new shoots. They shed their pollen copiously in May. The new female cones grow singly or in whorls of two to five round the tips of the shoots. They are pinkish, with the scales open to receive the pollen, and become rosy purple by June. By the following year they have become green, pointed ovoids in shape, five to eight centimetres (two to three inches) long, and with scales which are tightly closed. They subsequently become brown

and woody, and their scales open to release the winged seeds.

Black Poplar
Populus nigra var. *betulifolia*

Together with the Aspen this is the only other native poplar. It was common along the rivers of East Anglia and the Midlands in Medieval times, but it has been exploited almost out of existence. Specimens have been planted along the streets and in the playing fields of Cheshire and Lancashire, where it is known as the 'Manchester Poplar', but nowadays the quicker growing Black Italian hybrid poplars are planted in preference. They prefer good deep soils in moist lowlands.

It is a lofty, broad-domed tree which may attain thirty-five metres (115ft) in height. Its branches are massive, the

Black Poplar *Populus nigra* var. '*betulifolia*'

lowest originating low down on the trunk, and arching upwards before sweeping downwards to nearly touch the ground. The shoots grow upwards from the branches. The trunk is burry and the bark is impressively dark and coarsely fissured. The leaves are a pale brownish-green, becoming a deeper green, and are broad and delta-shaped, as those of the familiar Lombardy Poplar, of which this tree is another variety. The autumn colour is an attractive yellow.

Nowhere are the sexes close enough for propagation. In Morden Hall Park in south London, two fine specimens, male and female, are within 100m (330ft) of each other, and so far no seeds have naturally developed, although both trees flower abundantly. The male catkins are a brilliant red with the anthers protruding from behind the bract scales. The female catkins are firm and pale green, consisting of bract scales and styles with stigmas only. They appear in March before the leaves and, if fertilized, become fluffy with downy seed in June.

Aspen
Populus tremula
The Aspen was an early pioneer that took part in the colonizing of the raw soil following the retreat of the ice-sheets. Today it is common in the north by streams and in damp places, but more localized in the south where it spreads mainly by suckering, developing into stands and thickets of trees of one sex. The tree may attain a height of fifteen to twenty metres (fifty to sixty-five feet). The crown of a young tree is conical but as it grows older it becomes broken and slightly branched. The trunk often leans; the bark is greenish-grey and very smooth, with horizontal lenticels or pores.

The leaf is ovate to roundish in shape, dull green or greenish-grey above and paler beneath with shallow wavy margins. The leaf is attached to a very long, slender and flattened stalk (petiole), which allows the leaf to flutter even in the gentlest breeze, so maximizing evaporation. The autumn colour is a brilliant yellow. In common with all poplars, the sexes are separate. Male trees have thick grey-brown catkins which turn yellowish in mid-March. Female trees have green cat-

kins which become fluffy and white in May and later shed their fluffy seeds.

Crack Willow
Salix fragilis
The Crack Willow is considered to be a native, most probably occurring initially on the formerly undrained fens of East Anglia. From here it extended its range along the rivers of Britain, aided by the hand of Man. It was commonly planted along watercourses to stabilize the banks, and pollarded to ensure regular supplies of poles for fencing and other uses. The ease with which shoots can be broken off, or 'cracked', even by the wind, also ensured its spread downstream – a shoot or cutting will readily take root if embedded in wet soil. It also occurs commonly along ditches, and on any damp lowland spot where it has been planted or has sown itself by wind-blown seed.

Unlike most native willows which are shrubby, this species grows into a sizeable tree of up to twenty-six metres (eighty-five feet). The crown is broadly domed with heavy spreading branches late in life. The bark is a dull dark grey and scaly when young and develops thick brownish ridges later in life. The leaves are very long, lance-shaped and pendulous and are a rich glossy green. As in all willows, the sexes are separate. The male catkins are yellow and the female green, and both appear before the leaves.

Bay Willow
Salix pentandra
An uncommon native of North Wales and north of the Midlands, it is to be found on stream-sides or damp woodlands. It is a small tree, attaining a height of some ten to eighteen metres (thirty-three to sixty feet) high; the crown is domed on trees in the open, and the lower branches of old trees often rest on the ground. In woods, they grow tall and narrow. The leaves are a deep glossy green above, and, while narrower than those of the Goat Willow, they are broader and far less lance-like than those of the Crack Willow. The bark is brownish-grey and fissured with shallow orange cracks.

In most willows the catkins of both sexes appear before the leaves but in the Bay Willow they open bright yellow with

OPPOSITE:
Aspen *Populus tremula*

RIGHT:
Crack Willow *Salix fragilis*

BELOW:
Bay Willow *Salix pentandra*

OPPOSITE:
Goat Willow, Great Sallow, or Pussy Willow *Salix caprea*

the leaves in May or June. Pollen is carried by insects as well as being wind-borne. As the specific name *pentandra* implies, there are five or more stamens in the male flower.

Goat Willow or Great Sallow
Salix caprea

Often referred to with the Grey Willow as the Pussy Willow, the Goat Willow is a common native throughout Britain, growing by rivers and streams, and in damp situations in clearings and on woodland margins. Frequently it invades disturbed terrain such as disused quarries with flooded excavations, or waste ground. It is often shrub-like, but can also grow into a sizeable tree of some fifteen metres (fifty feet), with an open crown and crooked

stems. The bark is smooth and pale grey at first, later developing shallow brown fissures. It is the broadest leafed willow, the leaves being variably oval, more rounded at the base and short-pointed. The catkins appear from February to April, before the leaves. The catkins of the male trees are golden, while those of the female are erect and white with fluffy seeds by late May, prior to their wind-blown dispersal. Like the Grey Willow it does not strike well from cuttings.

Grey Willow
Salix cinerea
Like the Goat Willow commonly known as the 'Pussy Willow', the Grey Willow is a common native everywhere. It occurs in damp habitats like the Goat Willow too, the two species often growing in close proximity. However, the Grey Willow never attains much more than the size of a shrub, attaining a height of no more than six metres (twenty feet). The leaves are dark green above and whitish-green beneath with reddish-brown hairs, and are narrower than those of the Goat Willow, but still broad for willows. Small leafy stipules are present at the base of each leaf, a very useful identification characteristic.

Grey Willow *Salix cinerea*

Silver Birch
Betula pendula
The Silver Birch is a native pioneer of open land, as it was in early post-glacial times. It is nutritionally undemanding and thrives on the acid sandy soils of heaths, commons, clearings and margins of woods. It also flourishes on the acid peaty soils of moors and mountainsides, and in fact on any poor soils, such as that of disused railway sidings. A graceful, medium-sized but short-lived tree, it can grow up to twenty-seven metres (ninety feet) or more on a good soil. The crown shape is variable, but is usually tall and slender in young trees with upswept branches which end in long pendulous branchlets. Older trees are more broadly domed. It casts a light shade which allows some ground vegetation to grow underneath, and it can serve as nursery cover for forest and amenity trees. The bark of a very young tree is red-brown to orange, while that of a mature tree is smooth and white with black diamonds. In old trees it becomes fissured into small black knobbly plates, starting from the bottom of the trunk.

The leaves are sharply broad-shouldered at the base and acutely pointed, with sharply pointed margins. They unfurl emerald green and turn golden yellow in autumn. The yellow male catkins hang in tassels of two or three and release pollen in April. The erect pale green female catkins thicken and become pendulous before breaking up in autumn to shed their seed.

White or Downy Birch
Betula pubescens
The White Birch, like the Silver Birch, is a native from post-glacial times. Locally common, it is partial to ill-drained heaths, open country and valley bottoms. It is abundant in the Scottish highlands. Attaining a maximum height of twenty-five metres (eighty-two feet), its crown is irregular with twisting but not pendulous branches. The bark of a young tree starts red-brown, becoming a smooth greyish-white with horizontal grey bands, with no diamonds, as the tree grows older.

The leaves are smaller and more 'round-shouldered' at the base than those of the Silver Birch, with the widest part near the middle and not the base, as in the Silver Birch. The marginal teeth of the leaves are more evenly spaced than those of the Silver Birch and the undersides are covered with glistening white hairs; the leaves turn yellow in the autumn. The catkins are similar to those of the Silver Birch, with which it occasionally hybridizes.

Common Alder
Alnus glutinosa

The Common Alder, like the birches, is a native pioneer tree from early post-glacial times. It is common alongside both still and running water, in damp woods, along spring lines and in fenland. Alder woods are called fen carr, which, if left to develop naturally, consolidates the land for later planting of forest trees.

Reaching a height of twenty-five metres (eighty-two feet), the tree varies in shape, with a crown which may be broad, conical or pointed. Some trees become tall and gaunt through trying to reach the light in wood and carr. Initially the branches are ascending, but later become more horizontal. The bark is dark grey-brown, fissured into small squarish plates. The roots develop nodules caused by certain species of bacteria. These nodules capture

nitrogen from the pores of the soil, aiding the growth of the tree and ultimately increasing soil fertility.

The leaves are broadly rounded, often with an indentation at the tip, a useful identification characteristic. They are pale orange-brown when they open, but become dark green by the summer, and remain so until they fall in late autumn.

Alders are bisexual. The dark grey-

BELOW, LEFT:
White or Downy Birch
Betula pubescens

BELOW:
Silver Birch *Betula pendula*

purple male catkins give the tree a purple tinge in January, but they become dull yellow and pendulous by March and release their pollen in April. The smaller purple female catkins ripen to green ovoids which subsequently turn brown and woody after having shed their seeds.

Hornbeam
Carpinus betula

A native that arrived late, the Hornbeam did not travel very far north as a wild tree. This was probably due to the deteriorating weather conditions which set in after the climatic optimum of 6000 years ago. The Hornbeam makes heavy demands on nutrients from the soil and thrives best on heavy clay soils; it has formed woods in Essex, notably in Epping and Hainault, and in Hatfield Forest, as elsewhere in Hertfordshire and East Anglia. In Surrey and Kent it is a scattered component of the woods. It has been heavily pollarded in the past for charcoal and other uses (the wood is very hard), and is still a coppice tree, notably in Kent. It has been planted as a hedgerow tree in parks and gardens.

In some trees the crown is rounded and broadly domed, with ascending branches radiating from a short trunk, but in other trees, the trunk extends high into the crown. They may reach a height of thirty metres (100ft). The leaves could be mistaken for beech, but are much longer and toothed. Autumn colours are an attractive yellow to gold. The male and female catkins are borne on one tree. The male catkins are pendulous cylinders of overlapping yellow-green bract scales with orange stamens beneath, and are conspicuous in mass before they unfurl. The female flowers are leafy green bracts with the tips curled outwards. Under each are the red stigmas which catch the pollen. Later two nutlets develop.

Hazel
Corylus avellana

Hazel is a native shrub or small tree which forms the under-storey of many woodlands. In Boreal times it formed pure woods and provided the under-storey for the forests of Scots Pine which covered most of Britain. In recent times it has become an important component of hedgerows and an ubiquitous coppice shrub of oak woodland. It is rarely seen uncoppiced, a fact that could be regarded as a measure of the intensity of woodland management over the past centuries. However, coppicing declined as an industry over the first half of the twentieth century, as the common occurrence of neglected overgrown Hazel thickets indicates. Very recently coppicing has been revived, in order to let in light to encourage the return of the dormant spring flowers and also nesting birds, including nightingales.

The Hazel does not grow much over eight metres (twenty-five feet) and is a tall and multi-stemmed bush, sometimes growing from a short trunk, but usually from a coppice stool near to ground level. The bark is a shiny grey-brown with horizontal rows of pores and often with flaking strips. The leaves are broadest in the middle and measure six to seven centimetres (nearly three inches), are hairy to touch, and deep green turning to brown and finally yellow in the autumn.

The male catkins which hang in tassels of two or four, turn yellow in February and release their pollen in April in phase with the small bud-like female flowers with their red styles. The edible nuts are seated in cups or involucres of two overlapping bracts. They are green at first, and brown by autumn.

Common Beech
Fagus sylvatica
A common native of the south east and midlands of England, the Beech has been planted widely beyond this area. It thrives best on calcareous or sandy soils. There are impressive stands on the Chilterns and the North and South Downs, and it has been planted everywhere as a park tree for shelter belts, to form scenic clumps on hilltops, and in avenues and plantations.

One of our largest native species, it is a spreading tree in the open, often with heavy lower branches that touch the ground and afford the silvery grey smooth bark protection from the sun. In close woodland it can be tall and impressive, with clear trunks up to thirty metres (100ft) to the crown. It can grow up under other trees too but, having broken through the canopy, it shades out all competitors and most ground vegetation apart from mosses. On chalky soils it will

OPPOSITE, ABOVE:
Common Alder *Alnus glutinosa*

OPPOSITE, BELOW:
Hornbeam *Carpinus betula*

LEFT:
Hazel *Corylus avellana*

even overwhelm oaks and become the dominant forest tree. Its lifespan can be some 230 years. The root system is very shallow for such a large and heavy tree. This, combined with the density of the canopy, was the reason why beeches suffered so disastrously during the great storm of 16 October 1987 in south-east England.

The leaves are oval and slightly pointed, with silky hairs on the margins. Yellow-green in spring, light green in summer, they turn golden brown in autumn. The buds are slender and sharply pointed, with many light brown scales. Flowers of both sexes grow on the same tree. The male flowers are pale yellow rounded bunches of stamens on perpendicular stalks. Female flowers are bunches of styles protected by a cup of green bract scales. The triangular-sided shiny reddish-brown nuts or mast are enclosed in a four-lobed prickly husk, which splits open to release the nuts in autumn.

Sessile or Durmast Oak
Quercus petraea

One of the two native oaks, the Sessile Oak has a more westerly and northerly distribution than the English Oak. It is generally the dominant tree of the lighter acid soils of the hills, moorlands and mountains, but there is much hybridization where it overlaps with English Oak, including areas where pockets of this species occur in typical English Oak country in Kent, Surrey, Nottinghamshire and elsewhere. Such hybridization could possibly have started in prehistoric times, and may well be an example of evolution in action. The Sessile Oak appears the cleaner tree and not so susceptible to pests. Having adapted to slightly more austere environments it has a smaller associated fauna.

The trunk of the Sessile Oak in its pure form is straighter and the branches are more ascending than in the English Oak, and seldom, if ever, horizontal. It reaches a height of thirty to forty metres (100–130ft). The crown is domed but appears somewhat more open, due to the more even distribution of the leaves, which in the English Oak are arranged in dense rosettes. The bark of the Sessile Oak is grey and cracked and ridged into fine vertical plates. The leaves taper evenly from the petioles or stalks, which are long and yellowish; the leaves are dark green and paler beneath, turning yellow-brown in the autumn. The trees are bisexual, and the acorns are shorter than in the English Oak and are attached directly to the twig or by an extremely short stalk.

English or Pedunculate Oak
Quercus robur

The English Oak was the dominant native tree over wide areas of lowland Britain when forest almost totally covered the land in Atlantic times. It is still the dominant woodland tree everywhere on loamy or clay-based soils of plains and valleys, but can thrive on well-drained sandy soils. It is a commonly planted tree in hedgerows, parkland, gardens and town parks.

The oak is a generous host to a vast variety of plant and animal life, some beneficial, some harmful, but it is rugged enough to stay healthy. Marble-like wasp galls on the leaves (the familiar oak apple), and spangle galls underneath, are common infestations.

In the open the tree is wide-spreading with low, massive and often twisting branches. They can reach thirty-seven to forty metres (120–130ft) in height, and live to a great age. Some oaks in ancient parkland, where they have been protected over the centuries, for example in Richmond Park in London, are thought to be over 500 years old. Natural oak woodland is fairly open, allowing for a variety of ground vegetation, but in closed planta-

OPPOSITE, ABOVE:
Common Beech *Fagus sylvatica*

OPPOSITE, BELOW:
Sessile or Durmast Oak *Quercus petraea*

LEFT:
English Oak *Quercus robur*

tions the crowns are high up, and the trunks straight and almost branchless. The crown is unevenly domed. The rough bark· is grey and vertically fissured into short narrow plates.

The leaves are ovate, roundly lobed and varying in width, often tapering from the base upwards. Where they join the extremely short petiole or stalk, there is always a pair of auricles or small lobes. They are dark green, and paler beneath, and they turn a rich brown or orange-brown in autumn. The tree is bisexual, the fine yellow-green male catkins on short stems releasing pollen in May in phase with the minute globular pale brown female flowers with their red stigmas. The acorns are always attached to long stalks or peduncles.

Wych Elm
Ulmus glabra

The only certainly native elm, the Wych Elm is most probably the one that arrived with the oaks in Boreal times. It prefers good moist soils, usually on river banks, in damp hillside woods, and along small streams. Today it is found main-

ly in the west, and from Derbyshire northwards.

In closed canopies the Wych Elm has no definite shape, but is commonly a thin sinuously boled tree with the crown high up nearer the better light. Large Wych Elms can attain a height of forty metres (130ft) and may live for 230 years. Giant spreading trees, with broad crowns and crooked horizontal lower branches which occasionally touch the ground, are not uncommon in the open in sheltered fields, glens and valleys. This pattern was not unusual in southern England before Dutch Elm Disease struck, but is now rare. Young wild trees still strive to establish themselves in wooded situations.

The bark begins smooth and silvery grey, but becomes a network of deep, dark grey-brown ridges as the tree matures. The leaves are dark green and paler beneath and measure about twelve centimetres (five inches) long, very rough and with coarsely toothed margins and lopsided auricles or lobes at their bases, as in all elms. There are two leaf types, the common one, ovate and finely pointed, and the other, common in North Wales, abruptly shouldered towards the tip. The flowers are small dense green bunches with fine crimson stamens closely attached to the twigs. They include both sexual parts, the dark purplish-red stamens of the male and the white female styles. They are densely bunched together in round purplish tufts closely attached to the finer twigs. The seeds are clusters of membranous discs, each with a dark nutlet in its centre. In mass, they can give the tree a false leafy appearance in March and April, before the true leaves begin to open towards the end of April and May.

Smooth-leafed Elm
Ulmus carpinifolia

Many argue that this elm is a native of East Kent and East Anglia. Alternatively, it could have been introduced by two waves of pre-Iron Age invaders bringing with them two types of tree, one a small-leafed variety to Kent, the other a larger leafed variety to East Anglia. Prior to Dutch Elm Disease, it was a prevalent countryside tree in these areas, but is now uncommon. Elsewhere it occurs mainly as a planted tree. Large specimens can reach

OPPOSITE, ABOVE:
Smooth-leafed Elm *Ulmus carpinifolia*

OPPOSITE, BELOW:
Hawthorn or May Tree *Crataegus monogyna*

BELOW:
Wych Elm *Ulmus glabra*

a height of thirty metres (100ft) and their shape can vary from a tall high-crowned tree to a broad-crowned one. The finer outer branches are pendulous.

The leaves are smooth and leathery above, variably elliptical and oblique at the base, some being asymmetrical. New leaves are yellow-green, becoming shiny bright green above and turning yellow in the autumn. The flowers are dark red with white stigmas, and the seeds are bunches of green, notched discs with the nutlet near the notch. They make a fine display in February and March before the leaves unfold in May.

Hawthorn
Crataegus monogyna

A native thorny shrub and small tree known to have been part of the forest flora since Boreal times and to have increased as clearances proceeded. Now it occurs as a common woodland shrub and a colonizer of neglected land left to nature, commons, abandoned fields, and ungrazed downland, and is a major component of hedgerows everywhere. It is best known for its magnificent displays of white, pink-tinged blossom in May (it is also known as the 'May Tree') and its pleasant scent, and for the autumn crops of red berries. The tallest trees rarely exceed fifteen metres (fifty feet). The bark is smooth and dark orange or pinkish-brown, but becomes more rugged and fluted in older trees. The leaves are deep green and leathery, averaging three and a half centimetres (one and a half inches) long and are almost as broad as long. They are divided into three to seven lobes, the clefts developing variable depths towards the midrib, and each lobe is toothed or smoothly margined. They turn yellow-red or russet in the autumn. The flowers consist of five overlapping white petals, purple tipped stamens and one carpel with style. They are in dense clusters and are pollinated by insects.

The related Midland Hawthorn (*Crataegus oxyacantha*) is a native of central England and prefers woodland shade. It differs from *C monogyna* in that there are two or three stamens in the flower and hence two or three stones in the berry, whereas *C monogyna* usually has only one. The leaves taper from the base at a steeper

angle and they are less deeply and more roundly lobed. The cultivated form with a scarlet double flower, named 'Paul's Scarlet' after the attractive climbing rose, is planted in cities and suburbia.

Mountain Ash or Rowan
Sorbus aucuparia

Together with the Juniper, the Rowan is a survivor of the glaciations. It grows as an isolated tree or in groups of dispersed trees in open woodland or on woodland fringes everywhere, preferring sandy or lighter soils. It is also a tree of the mountains, to be found up to 900m (3000ft) in altitude, and can even gain a footing on ledges of crags, no doubt distributed by birds.

It is a small- to medium-sized tree, attaining fifteen to twenty metres (fifty to sixty-five feet), usually with steeply ascending branches and an irregular domed crown. The bark is smooth and silver grey. The leaves are pinnate, ie each one comprises a series of opposed lance-like leaflets along a common stem with a single terminal leaflet. They are deep green above and greyish-green beneath and rarely change colour before falling, except in Wester Ross and Sutherland where the autumn leaves are a spectacular scarlet. The small flowers grow in creamy-white inflorescences about ten to twelve centimetres (four to five inches) across. They open in May, and ripen to clusters of orange berries by July, which turn scarlet within a few days. It is widely planted as an ornamental tree.

Wild Service Tree
Sorbus torminalis

The Wild Service Tree is a very uncommon native woodland tree occurring in scattered localities as far north as Cumbria. It thrives best on clay-based soils, most particularly where there is underlying chalk as on the North Downs, but also in moist spots on the adjacent greensands. Other notable situations are in Ham Street Woods near Romney Marsh in Kent, the Wyre Forest and woods of the Pennine limestone. Its occurrence is an indication of ancient woodland undisturbed by the plough. It is a medium-sized tree of up to twenty-three metres (seventy-five feet). Within woodland it can be a narrowish tree with a high crown, whereas in less shaded locations it tends to be wider with a broader crown. The bark is very dark grey, broken into small scaly plates.

The leaves are lobed and maple-like, but not opposed as in maples, and the lower pair of lobes is wide and wing-like. They are hard, shiny and deep green both above and below and they turn orange-red or purple in the autumn. The sprays of white flowers with yellow stamens appear in May, and these develop into hard green speckled berries, which subsequently ripen to reddish-brown.

Whitebeam
Sorbus aria

The Whitebeam is a native of the woodlands on the chalk and limestone hills of southern England. It is a medium-sized tree, up to nineteen metres (sixty feet) high. In the open, it is a compact tree until old age, often with the trunk dividing low down into two or more major branches,

OPPOSITE:
Wild Service Tree *Sorbus torminalis*

BELOW:
Mountain Ash or Rowan *Sorbus aucuparia*

but the crown is neatly and regularly domed and internally dense with branchlets. The main branches are steeply angled, more so towards the top of the tree, and the crown terminates evenly. In dense yew woods, the crowns are raised to the better light on long and sometimes sinuous trunks, which occasionally have vertical, spiral splits in the bark. There is often thick sucker growth around the base. Its bark is smooth and light grey, occasionally coppery, and sometimes with long irregular fissures.

The leaves are roundly elliptical and pointed, the margins variably serrated, and the undersides white and pubescent. Leaf colour is dark green above and whitish green beneath, and a light ochre in autumn. The white shimmering effect of the leaves fluttering in a breeze shows off the trees to good effect, for example against the dark green of yews, and the lighter greens of oak and beech on wooded downland slopes. The small flowers open into heads of creamy white in May, and develop into showy clusters of orange berries by July, which turn red by early August.

Crab Apple
Malus sylvestris

The Crab Apple is a native found almost everywhere in woods, hedgerows, and overgrown commons and roadsides. Of small size, not usually attaining a height of more than ten metres (thirty-three feet), it is a broad-domed, unevenly crowned, and often lop-sided tree with dense twisting branches. Trees in closed woods can be taller and narrower. The shoots are often thorny and pointed, a characteristic never present in those with a cultivated ancestry which have escaped to the wild, which also have pinker flowers. The bark is dark brown and cracked into small plates.

The leaves are variably ovate, pointed and often oblique at the base and have forward-toothed margins. They are deep green above and whitish and pubescent beneath. The five-petalled flowers are white, sometimes faintly tinged with pink, with yellow stamens, and are borne on downy stalks from short stems. The fruits are globular, glossy, yellow or yellow-green apples with white spots, some becoming flushed with red in the autumn,

averaging two and a half centimetres (one inch) across.

Wild Cherry or Gean
Prunus avium

A fairly common native tree, the Wild Cherry is frequent in many areas. It thrives best on chalk or limestone-based soils, and clays overlying chalk, especially in clearings and margins of oak and beech woods. It is a short-lived, fast-growing tree with branches arranged in a whorl-like series up the trunk, as, for example, in many conifers. The crown is regularly conical in younger trees, and broadens out in older ones. In closed woods, some trees develop clean, straight trunks up to the crown which may be twenty-two metres (seventy-two feet) or more above the ground. The bark is smooth and shiny, copper or bronze colour, with pale lenticels or pores in banks.

The leaves are pointed and variably oval to spear-shaped. The margins are serrated by forward pointing teeth, the broadest part being in the middle or nearer to the tip. There are paired glands at the base. They are fresh green above and paler below and turn yellow or crimson in the autumn. The large white flowers grow in sprays on long stems, and in April and May give magnificent displays of white blossom. The cherries ripen to dark red by August. There is a cultivated strain with double flowers called 'Plena', very heavily blossomed, which has returned to the wild as an escape.

Bird Cherry
Prunus padus

A native with a northern distribution, the Bird Cherry grows along stream banks. It is common in Scotland, and local along streams of the Pennine limestone. It can reach a height of fifteen metres (fifty feet) and the crown is conical at first, but older trees become more rounded, losing their shape as the branches droop. The bark is smooth and dark grey-brown, with an odour of bitter almonds. The leaves are leathery, light glossy green above and paler underneath, turning pale yellow or red in autumn. In shape they are broadly elliptical and are often broadest near the pointed tip. The margins are finely toothed.

OPPOSITE, ABOVE LEFT:
Crab Apple *Malus sylvestris*

OPPOSITE, ABOVE RIGHT:
Wild Cherry Tree or Gean *Prunus avium*

OPPOSITE, BELOW:
Whitebeam *Sorbus aria*

The individual flowers are small and densely packed around the stem of the inflorescence into showy white spikes, which are at their best shortly after the leaves open in late April and early May. They are very fragrant. The small bitter fruits are green at first but ripen to dark purple or shiny black.

Box
Buxus sempervirens

A native broadleaved evergreen, and a late arrival before Britain was isolated by the sea, the Box extended its range as a wild tree no further than southern England. It was formerly widespread over the chalk and limestone hills, but the demands of the printing trade (Box was used for making engravings) depleted the natural stocks until there are now only a few scattered natural stands in Gloucestershire, the Chilterns, Kent and, notably, the Box Hill area in Surrey. It thrives best in the shade and occurs mainly as undershrub in beech woods where it grows from dense scrub to rangy trees with sinuous branches, to six and a half metres (twentyone feet) high. The crowns are untidy, some being pendulous and often lopsided, while others are raggedly spire-like. Unlike wild trees, cultivated trees are neat and compact and lend themselves to being trained by topiarists into dense hedges and more ambitious shapes. The light brownish-grey bark is finely fissured into shallow wavy vertical plates.

The leaves are arranged in opposed pairs along the stem and are small, elliptical, smooth and leathery. They are glossy dark green above and paler below. The tiny yellow-green flowers, which open in April, are clustered in the bases of the leaves. They are unusual because the male and female flowers are separate, but in the same inflorescences, the single female with four styles in the centre being surrounded by five or six male flowers. The fruit is a globose three-horned capsule.

Holly
Ilex aquifolium

A native tree, the Holly is common everywhere as under-storey in woods, particularly of oak and beech. It occurs on many different soils wherever birds have

OPPOSITE, ABOVE:
Bird Cherry *Prunus padus*

OPPOSITE, BELOW:
Holly *Ilex aquifolium*

Box *Buxus sempervirens*

voided the seeds, for example along streams, on mountainsides, alongside roads, and commonly in hedgerows where it was initially planted as trees. In heavy shade it bears no fruit and develops a straggly shape in its efforts to reach the light. However in good light it begins as a conical or spire-shaped tree, becoming fuller and denser with upcurved branches as it matures. Older trees lose this shape and become pendulous. It can reach twenty-two metres (seventy-two feet) in height. The bark is pinkish or silvery green with warts on older trees.

The leaves are hard, glossy and dark green above and paler underneath. In mature trees the lower leaves are buckled and spiny, whereas above two and a half metres (seven feet) they become spineless and elliptical – possibly an evolutionary response to browsing animals over the ages. The flowers are small, globular and tightly clustered around the stem on the bases of the leaves. They open white and are fragrant in May. Only the female trees bear berries, the clusters of which ripen to scarlet by October and are often eaten by redwings and fieldfares in hard winters.

Field Maple *Acer campestre*

Field Maple
Acer campestre

The only native maple, the Field Maple is common as a wayside tree and hedgerow shrub in chalk and limestone country in southern England, its range extending northwards to Staffordshire and Derbyshire. It is a medium sized tree, attaining a height of twenty-three metres (seventy-five feet). It is either broadly domed or narrow with a high dome. The bark is pale brown or dark grey with fine cracks and pale ridges.

The leaves open pinkish or reddish in April, then turn light green and eventually dark green. They are five lobed, the top lobe being pointed, while the bottom pair are smaller. The autumn colours are bright yellow, and sometimes red and dark purple in trimmed hedgerow trees. The flowers open with the leaves as creamy hermaphrodite clusters in April/May and the fruits are two pairs of winged seeds joined in the centre. The wings are always horizontal, light green and stained crimson.

Large-leafed Lime
Tilia platyphyllos

Considered a native but possibly an early pre-Roman introduction, the Large-leafed Lime is now rare as a wild tree. The most notable localities for natural stands are on the limestone of the Wye Valley near Chepstow and in Yorkshire. It occurs widely as a planted tree in parks, along avenues and roadsides and is also planted in towns in preference to the Common Lime because it is a cleaner tree.

Trees may reach a height of thirty-two metres (105ft). The crown is bowl-shaped in young trees, and it grows usually into a tall, narrow-domed tree with steeply ascending branches. It is rarely a spreading tree. The trunk is usually clear and free of epicormic sprouts and the bark is dark grey and finely cracked or with small flat ridges.

The leaves are broad and heart-shaped, rounded but sharp-pointed, and very angled at the base. The leaf stalks are hairy and the upper surface is pubescent. The leaves are up to fifteen centimetres (six inches) long and the same in width. They are light green and hairy, with white or orange tufts in the vein axils. The yellowish-white flowers hang in pendulous clusters of three or four and are attached by a common stalk to a green strap-like bract. The small nut-like fruits of eight to ten millimetres (nearly half an inch) across are ribbed and hairy. At this time the bract turns brown, and it assists with the seed dispersal.

Small-leafed Lime
Tilia cordata
The Small-leafed Lime is a native tree which arrived late: it spread no further than Cumbria and did not reach Ireland. It was formerly a common forest tree, dominant locally until Saxon times. Its decline was due in part to Man having no

Large-leafed Lime *Tilia platyphyllos*

RIGHT:
Small-leafed Lime *Tilia cordata*

BELOW:
Common Lime *Tilia X europaea*

further use for its long bark fibres for ropes and clothing, and in part to grazing animals. These factors have reduced its presence as a wild tree to a few woods in scattered localities, including the Avon Gorge, the Wye Valley, and Wyre Forest in Warwickshire. It has also survived above streams and sheltered cliffs in Wales and the Pennine limestone hills. It is more frequently seen as a tree planted along avenues and roads, in parks and in gardens.

The tree may grow very tall, up to thirty-two metres (105ft) high. The crown is irregularly domed and densely foliaged, the branches becoming pendulous and casting heavy shadows. Young trees are conical. The bark is dark grey, finely fissured, and on older trees sometimes ribbed. The leaves are smaller than in other limes, blue-green, hairless, roundish and cordate (heart-shaped) at the base. They are also more abruptly and finely pointed. There are reddish tufts in the vein axils on the underside.

The small flowers are white and arranged in starry clusters on firm stalks which project at all angles from the dark foliage. As in all limes the flower stalk is attached about halfway along a long leaf-like bract which eventually turns brown. The flowers of all limes are 'perfect', that is, comprising a female ovule surrounded by male stamens, all contained within a corolla of petals. The small green globular fruit of this species is hard, slightly prickly and without ridges.

Common Lime
Tilia X europaea (syn. T vulgaris)
A natural hybrid between *Tilia cordata* and *T platyphyllos*, the Common Lime's seeds rarely germinate in Britain, and it spreads by suckers. Nonetheless it is probably a native, its pollen having been identified in peat formed in Atlantic times. It may have subsequently died out in Britain, to be reintroduced from Europe long ago, the first recorded introductions being in the early 1600s. It is now a commonly planted tree of avenues, streets, parks, churchyards and village greens, with a fairly general distribution.

Some of these trees are at least 400 years old. It grows into a very lofty tree, one of the tallest, up to forty metres (130ft) in height. In shape it is often narrow and high-domed, but it can also be billowing and multi-domed, as in many specimens the trunk divides into two or more vertical and slanting limbs. The main branches are typically ascending and arching, sometimes bent. Others are horizontal and inclined to droop at lower levels, particularly on older trees which may have massive lower branches. The trunks of mature trees are almost invariably dense at their bases with sprouting leaves, which often extend up to the crown, which itself may be bedecked with mistletoe. Sucker growth commonly adds to the foliage congestion at the base of the tree.

The bark is dull grey and smooth in young trees, and later becomes rough with fine cracks or a network of shallow ridges. Burrs are common. The light green, hairless leaves are variable in size, but smaller than those of *T platyphyllos* and larger than those of *T cordata*. There are six to eight pairs of opposed veins, and white tufts of hair on the underside in the angles they make with the midrib. The stalks or petioles are long and hairless. The leaves become very sticky with the honey-dew of aphids in July. The flowers are fragrant and very attractive to insects. They are 'perfect' flowers, complete with carpel, stamens and delicate pale yellow to white petals. They hang in clusters of four to six from a common stalk attached to a pale strap-like bract, which turns brown by the time the fruits have formed. The fruits are nut-like, faintly ribbed and very hairy.

Common Ash
Fraxinus excelsior

A common native tree found everywhere, the Common Ash prefers moist base-rich soils, occurring as a wild and planted countryside tree in hedgerows, hillside woods, on roadsides and in formerly suburban situations. Wild woods are to be found mainly on the limestone of the Cotswolds, Derbyshire and Yorkshire. It has commonly been pollarded, and is still coppiced commercially. It frequently appears in developing woodland as a pioneering tree. Specimens have attained an age of at least 230 years, and it grows into a lofty tree, some forty metres (130ft) in height, with steeply angled sinuous branches, the lower ones originating rela-tively low down on the main trunk, resulting in a broad-domed or flat-topped tree. Straight-trunked trees do occur. In woodland the canopy is open due to the lightness of the foliage. The bark is pale grey and smooth in saplings, but later develops a network of ridges. It is usually the last tree to produce its pinnate leaves, in June. Leaves may turn yellow for a brief period in autumn, but may fall while still green due to severe frost.

Dense clusters of purple flowers cover the tree in April before the leaves open. The trees are variably all male or all female, or both. Not only that, individual trees sometimes alternate sexes. 'Perfect' flowers are known, but are exceptional. The seed is embedded in the base of a single long leafy vane called a key. The keys hang in green bunches in July and turn brown by autumn, when some are scattered by the winds, but on many trees they persist throughout the winter, falling when the new growth begins.

Common Ash *Fraxinus excelsior*

POSSIBLE NATIVES OR EARLY INTRODUCTIONS

Grey Poplar
Populus canescens

The Grey Poplar is possibly a native, or it may have been introduced at the same time as the White Poplar by early immigrants. It is intermediate in many significant respects between the Aspen and White Poplar, and is probably an ancient natural hybrid of the two. It occurs most commonly in fields, commons, spinneys and along rivers in the wide chalk and limestone valleys of southern England, and is planted on poor soils inland and along low coasts for shelter and to consolidate the soil.

Due possibly to hybrid vigour, it develops into a spreading, massive-limbed giant with multiple domes, with the bole running high up in the tree before the main branching starts. Its lifespan is more than 200 years, and it can grow up to thirty-eight metres (125ft) or more in height. The bark is generally similar to that of the White Poplar, but a darker grey.

The leaves vary in shape between roundly elliptical with big, curved but shallow marginal teeth (similar to the Aspen), to shallowly lobed leaves, somewhat angularly shouldered at the base (resembling the White Poplar). The undersides are whitish and felt-like, greyer than in White Poplar but still providing a good shimmering effect in early summer. Newly opened leaves and sucker leaves can easily be mistaken for those of the White Poplar. The trees are male or female. The male trees spread by suckering and the male catkins are silky and grey to reddish-purple, lengthening to three to four centimetres (nearly one and a half inches) in March. In April they are yellow until the pollen is shed. Females are rarely planted due to the masses of fluffy seed they release in July.

White Poplar
Populus alba

An early introduction in prehistoric times, the White Poplar was probably valued for its quick growth and ability to sucker freely on poor and loose soils. For this reason, it has been planted on a large scale along low coastlines, especially behind sand-dunes to assist in the stabilization of wind-blown soils. Inland it is local in well-watered valleys and lowlands, where it occurs in hedgerows, woods and road verges, and is much planted in parks and towns. It can grow up to twenty-five metres (eighty-two feet) high near rivers, but is a short-lived tree. The bark of the lower trunk is grey-green, furrowed, and disrupted by cracking and pitting, whereas the upper trunk and branches are smooth and silvery or creamy white, and pitted with small black diamonds. The tree is broadest near the top with twisted branches, the lower ones level or drooping, and it invariably leans to one side.

The upper surfaces of the leaves are dark greyish-green, and the undersides are brilliant white with felt-like hairs. This, in mass, gives the tree a shimmering effect, greatly enhanced in a breeze when viewed in sunlight against dark clouds. The mature leaf is typically five-lobed, the lobe furthest from the petiole or stalk

OPPOSITE, ABOVE:
White Willow *Salix alba*

OPPOSITE, BELOW:
White Poplar *Populus alba*

BELOW:
Grey Poplar *Populus canescens*

being the longest, and the middle pair the widest. The base of the leaf is truncate or rounded. The trees are either male or female, the male catkins being grey or crimson tassels which come out in April before the leaves. The female catkins are yellowish-green, becoming fluffy with seed down in July.

White Willow
Salix alba

Probably a native, and with a more southerly distribution than the Crack Willow, and more local in distribution. It is a tree of the river sides and damp places of lowland areas. The seeds require damp soil for germination, but they are widely planted.

They grow to about twenty-five metres (eighty-two feet), but many trees of that height are senile hulks, having lost

branches during storms after some sixty or seventy years of life. The crown may be tall or broad and billowing, usually with the main branches ascending; the finer branches can be pendulous. The bark is dark or blue-grey and cracked into vertical ridges or a network of thick ridges on the main trunk, becoming smoother and pockmarked higher up the tree, but the cracking is overall on very old trees.

The leaves are narrow, lance-like and pointed, five to eight millimetres (quarter of an inch) long, and are finely toothed around the margins. They are covered with velvety hairs and are blue-grey above and white underneath. A white scintillating effect occurs when the wind disturbs the leaves and reveals the undersides. Usually the leaves are smaller than those of the Crack Willow.

The catkins are four to six centimetres (one and a half to two and a half inches) long and appear in April. The male catkins are yellow, the female catkins green and become fluffy with seed-down in June.

Trees are either female or male. The pollen is both wind and insect-borne, the insects being attracted by the nectar glands in the flowers. It hybridizes easily with the Crack Willow and there are many cultivars, including the Silver, Coral-bark and Cricket-bat Willows.

English Elm
Ulmus procera

Probably not a native, the English Elm was perhaps introduced by pre-Iron Age tribes from Europe. It imparted, before the catastrophe of Dutch Elm Disease, a certain evocative English character to the rural landscape. Its distribution extended over the plains and valleys of central and southern England as far north as Yorkshire, westwards to the Usk Valley and Dartmoor, and eastwards to Canterbury. There are still exceptional protected areas where English Elms survive, such as the coastal strip between the South Downs and the English Channel. Of these the Brighton area was the most notable until the great storm of 16 October 1987 greatly reduced the remaining Elm population.

It is a lofty tree, with a long straight trunk, which can attain a height of thirty-eight metres (125ft) and an age of 300 years. The branches are well spaced and sinuous, each terminating in a dense profusion of dark green foliage. The final branching of the upper bole terminates in the dense dome of the upper canopy. The general appearance suggests a billowing dome, with one or more 'waists' between the billowing skirts below. The bole itself is often dense with sprouting foliage. The bark is dark brown or grey, deeply cracked into vertical plates.

The leaves are variable, four to ten centimetres (one and a half to four inches) long, rough and leathery, roundish or ovoid, and pointed, with ten to twelve pairs of veins, and oblique at the base. In autumn they turn yellow or yellowish-orange. The flowers are dark red tufts of stamens on short shoots, which give a subtle display of colour in March, and develop into clusters of rounded, green membranous discs in April before the leaves open in May. Each disc contains a seed which is usually infertile. English Elms propagate by suckers, which can spread along a hedgerow.

English Elm *Ulmus procera*

Wild Pear
Pyrus communis

A doubtful native, the Wild Pear was probably introduced in prehistoric times. The pure wild form probably no longer exists, but strains very similar to it can be found growing in hedgerows, wood margins and other wild places. They are descendants of hybrids between the original wild pear and other species from southern Europe, which were propagated for larger and sweeter fruit; some could be throwbacks showing the main characteristics of the original tree. There is a pure wild species, *Pyrus cordata*, that grows in south-west England.

It is a small to medium-sized tree of up to ten metres (thirty-three feet) in height, with a straight and usually clean bole, surmounted by a high, conical or rounded crown, sometimes lop-sided, with ascending branches. The extremities of the lower ones droop somewhat. The finer branches are often twisted and confused. The bark is blackish and cracked into small squares.

The leaves open in May. They are a glossy green, pointed, and elliptical or roundly ovate. The heads of white flowers blossom profusely in April, mainly before the opening of the leaves. The small fruits are edible and apple- or pear-shaped, green and finely spotted brown at first, but turning completely brown by August. Many shoots are thorny.

Wild Pear *Pyrus communis*

INTRODUCED TREES WHICH HAVE BECOME NATURALIZED

Certain species of introduced trees, at least a dozen, have now established themselves as wild trees, some locally and others widely. Sycamore, which can seed itself on almost any soil and can suppress other vegetation, has become a common woodland tree, and is often mistaken for a native tree. Other more exotic trees can seed themselves if local conditions are favourable, but established local native vegetation usually keeps them in check.

Maritime Pine
Pinus pinaster

A native tree along the coasts of the central and western Mediterranean, the Maritime Pine was introduced into Britain prior to 1596. There are a few specimen trees in arboreta in the south but most trees are in plantations and woods in south-west Surrey, Hampshire and, particularly, along the coast from central Bournemouth to Branksome Park. Here they grow wild in small woods on the slopes and tops of the sandy cliffs, and spread inland into private gardens. They prefer a light, well-drained, shady soil, and are planted to stabilize sand-dunes.

The crown is often on a tall, lean trunk, which is usually slightly curved near the base, but branches can grow quite low on the trunk. Trees reach an average height of twenty-eight metres (ninety-two feet). The bark is deep purple, blackish or reddish. On older trees it is cracked into small, squarish and shiny plates. The pale green needle-like leaves are in bundles of two and are slightly twisted. They are the longest of the pine leaves, measuring up to twenty-two centimetres (nearly nine inches) long.

The male flowers are yellow-orange catkins clustering around the new shoots. The pollen is shed in June to fertilize the crimson female flowers, which are clustered in whorls around the tips of the shoots or halfway along. The cones average fifteen centimetres (six inches) long, but can be much longer. They cluster in whorls of two or three and many remain along the branches for years before the scales open. They are long and tapering with bright, shiny brown scales, each tipped centrally on a knob with a vicious down-curved spine. Many trees in the Bournemouth area are self-seeding, and vigorous saplings are already producing cones and forming a natural under-storey.

European Larch
Larix decidua

The European Larch is a native of the Alps of central Europe, and there are outlying relict populations elsewhere, including Czechoslovakia and hills in the Polish plain. It was first introduced into Britain as an ornamental tree in about 1620, and was planted locally for quick timber in Scotland during the 1700s, notably by the Dukes of Atholl in the Spey Valley. Today it is a commonplace tree of the countryside, occurring particularly in forestry plantations, where its light shade and good leaf litter allow the healthy growth of wild flowers and other wildlife. They are also planted as shelter-belts, in

OPPOSITE:
Maritime Pine *Pinus pinaster*

BELOW:
European Larch *Larix decidua*

roadside spinneys, as pheasant coverts, and as ornamental trees in parks and gardens.

It is a graceful conical tree when young with mainly ascending branches, but horizontal branches are also common and the lower branches are often descending. They arch gracefully upwards at their extremities. In close stands, the trunks are clean and straight up to the high crowns in the canopy. However, trees growing in the open lose some of their branches, and those remaining often become stout and horizontal, so that the tree loses its pyramidal shape and becomes spreading. They may grow to a height of forty to forty-five metres (130-148ft). Initially the bark is grey to greenish-brown and smooth, but it cracks vertically later.

The leaves are soft, delicate needles, set singly and spirally on new shoots, and arranged in rosettes of twenty to thirty on short spurs on older shoots. They are two to three centimetres (about an inch) long, emerge emerald green in March, darken during the summer, and become golden yellow before the autumn. Most foliage hangs from the main branches on long pendulous shoots, which are festooned with strings of female cones and also, on vigorous trees, with minute whitish or yellow male flowers in spring.

The young female cones are one centimetre (half an inch) long and very flower-like, with their rose-red, scarlet or whitish, open scales in spring. Later they become tight egg-like cones with green rounded scales, sometimes tinged with purple, with blunt tips that are straight or sometimes turned inwards when the cones

Common Walnut *Juglans regia*

have become brown or woody by the autumn. Out-turned tips are rare, and such a flaring outwards is usually an indication of hybridization with Japanese Larch, a common occurrence in the countryside today. Cones can be up to two to four centimetres (one to one and a half inches) long. Self-seeding occurs in the wild.

Common Walnut
Juglans regia

Native from the Balkans to China, the Common Walnut has been cultivated in Britain possibly since Roman times. Between the fifteenth and nineteenth centuries walnut trees were cultivated for their hard wood, suitable for gunstocks, as well as for their crops of nuts. Now they occur quite commonly as ornamental trees on farms, in parks, gardens and as wayside trees. Over the years they have escaped into the wild and are seen occasionally in woods, hedgerows and on neglected land. The Common Walnut is widely distributed, being commonest in the south and south west, and scarce in northern Scotland.

The crown is widely spreading, and the tree may attain a height of twenty-two metres (seventy-two feet) and an age of 200 years. The branches are long and sinuous, the smaller ones twisted and bunched. In ancient trees the branches are massive and often horizontal. The smaller twigs are hollow, but partitioned by strands of pith. Externally, the twigs are dark brown and bear squat black buds in winter. The bark is very light grey and smooth at first, but becomes deeply furrowed in old age.

The leaves are alternately arranged and pinnate, and twenty to forty centimetres (eight to sixteen inches) in length. They are made up of three or four pairs of opposite stalkless leaflets on a common stem with a terminal leaflet, which is the longest. The side pairs diminish towards the base, and average eight by four centimetres (three by one and a half inches). The leathery oblong leaves with pointed tips open orange-brown in late April to early May, and by June become dull green above with yellow veins, and yellowish-green underneath. Male catkins are green and later purple on the last year's wood. The female flowers are small, green flask-shaped ovaries with feathery orange-yellow styles, on the ends of new shoots. The fruit are green globular drupes three to four centimetres (nearly two inches) long, which contain the convoluted two-valved husk or shell, which further contains the double brain-like kernel where the cotyledons or food leaves are situated.

Sweet or Spanish Chestnut
Castanea sativa

The Sweet or Spanish Chestnut is a native of the eastern Mediterranean and Asia Minor. The Romans were responsible for its spread through Europe and its introduction to Britain. Further introductions occurred and the tree has been established here for many centuries. It grows more vigorously and abundantly in southern England, but there are notable fine old Scottish trees. It was coppiced intensively in some areas, but this activity has declined, although it is still maintained on a reduced scale for split paling fences. Those which have escaped into the wild are most numerous in these areas. Otherwise it occurs in most regions in woods, copses and especially in the surrounds of

Sweet or Spanish Chestnut *Castanea sativa*

country estates and urban gardens. It has, to a limited extent, established itself as a wild species through the aid of jays and squirrels.

Young trees are conical and open with the branches set in whorls. Older trees become columnar with rounded tops. Very old trees are widely spreading, with multiple domes and twisted upper branches, the lower branches massive and often touching the ground. They can reach a height of thirty-five metres (115ft) and an age of 450 years. The bark in young trees is smooth and silvery grey, but in more mature trees it becomes grey or brown and cracked into ridges and plates. In older trees it becomes spirally twisted.

The leaves are serrated on the margins and attached alternately along the stems. They are oblong with pointed tips. When they unfold in May they are bronze, but turn to a dark glossy green by July. In October they become pale yellow. They are connected to the shoot by red or yellow stalks. There are eighteen to twenty parallel veins each side of the leaf, each extending into a bristle tooth.

The male and female flowers are separate, but are grouped on the same slender filamentous catkins, growing from the axils (upper angles) of the leaves. The male flowers consist of dense tufts of light yellow stamens and crowd the major portion of the catkin from the tip downwards. The female flowers occupy the base, but also form their own separate, spreading catkins of five to six flowers. Each flower comprises a bunch of slender white styles protruding from a rosette of minute bright green spines about one centimetre (half an inch) across. Although the pollen is windborne, insects are attracted by the scent and act as pollinators. The fruit, the edible shiny reddish-brown chestnut, is protected inside a prickly light green husk, which splits into four lobes in autumn to release the two to three edible nuts, distinguished by one flattened side.

Turkey Oak
Quercus cerris

A native of southern Europe from France to the Balkans, the Turkey Oak was introduced and raised by J Luccombe, an Exeter nurseryman, in 1735. It is a fast-growing tree on all well-drained soils. Today it is a fairly common countryside tree. It is also a widespread ornamental tree, found in deer parks, country estates, town parks and along roadsides. It has little commercial value. It seeds itself easily, and has established itself widely as a wild tree in woodlands in southern England.

It grows into a lofty, widely spreading tree up to forty metres (130 feet) high, and trees over 200 years old around Exeter are still vigorous. It has long, straight ascending main branches, arising from a stout, relatively short main trunk. The bark is rough and dark grey, with fine, deep, vertical fissures.

The leaves are usually long and narrow, but sometimes long and ovate. They are lobed like those of English Oak, but the lobes are more pointed or triangular. Also they are darker green and shiny, but paler and woolly underneath. In autumn the leaves turn a rich orange brown. The stalks are hairy and about two centimetres (one inch) long. The buds are brown and surrounded by long twisted scales.

The male flowers are pendulous catkins of fine crimson flowers that turn yellow

Turkey Oak *Quercus cerris*

before releasing their pollen in June. The female flowers are in the axils of new leaves, and are ovoid in shape, occurring singly or in clumps of two or three. The red stigmas protrude from delicate yellowish-pink scales. The stalkless acorns are long and the cups deep and mossy, covered in narrow, greyish-fawn scales.

Holm Oak
Quercus ilex

A native of the western Mediterranean and the Iberian peninsula, the Holm Oak has been planted in Britain for over 400 years and is the most common of our evergreen oaks. It is a sombre-looking, bushy tree found in cemeteries, large Victorian gardens, parks and sea-fronts of the south and west coasts of England. The density and toughness of its foliage make it ideal for its role as shelter-belt tree. It prefers the warmer summers of the south and west, and has established itself locally as a wild tree. It occurs as a planted tree as far north as Scotland, where there are some notable giant trees. In prolonged frosts the leaves become seared and die, but they are replaced by new growth from dormant axial buds in the summer.

The crown is typically dense, dark and broadly domed, often on a short main trunk which branches into several ascending limbs reaching heights up to thirty metres (100ft). Trees of at least 300 years are known. In mature trees, the bark is dark grey and cracked into fine square plates.

The new leaves unfold silvery white in June, but soon turn shiny blackish-green

Holm Oak *Quercus ilex*

above and retain their dull fawn and felt-like undersides. In young trees the leaves are broad, elliptical and spiny, but in old trees they become longer, lance-like and without spines. Trees of intermediate age have both types of leaf.

The male flowers are minute, feathery clumps of stamens along a thread-like catkin. They turn from green to yellow when it is time to release pollen in June. The female flowers are minute green clusters in which the acorns develop. The mature acorns are on very short stems and are embedded in a scaly, felt-like cup. They are minute compared with the acorns of English Oak.

False Acacia, Robinia or Locust Tree
Robinia pseudoacacia

This tree is not a true acacia, but a member of the pea family (Leguminosae). It is native to the Appalachian Mountains and the middle Mississippi Valley, but is now more widespread in North America. It was introduced into Britain by John Tradescant in 1638, and was a favourite tree of William Cobbett. He planted them by the thousand between 1810 and 1830 in preference to oaks, because of their faster growth and hardy enduring wood. Locust Trees are now common everywhere south of the Midlands. They prefer light, sandy

False Acacia, Robinia or Locust Tree *Robinia pseudoacacia*

soils and are often planted to stabilize shifting sands along the coast. Also, they improve sterile soils by virtue of the nitrogen-fixing nodules that cluster on the roots.

The crown is open and broadest near the top, with twisted branches and a short trunk, which often develops into two or more steeply ascending main trunks. The tree can attain a height of thirty metres (100ft) and can live for 250 years or more, although most die much younger. The bark is smooth and a rich brown. As the tree ages it becomes a dull grey, and the trunk becomes fluted with cracks developing into deep ridges. Burrs are also present on old trees.

The leaves are alternate and pinnate, mainly pendulous and fifteen centimetres (six inches) long. They contain thirteen to fifteen pairs of oval leaflets with a single terminal one, all on short stalks and attached to a common stem. They are entire except for minute notches or spines on the rounded blunt-pointed tips. They open a bright yellow, turning yellow-green above and later hairy beneath. There are short paired spines adjacent to each bud, and winter scale buds are absent, the compressed undeveloped leaves being hidden in the bases of the leaf stems. There are no autumn colours, but a small garden cultivar 'Frisia', which originated in Holland, grows golden summer leaves which turn orange in autumn.

The white pea-like flowers are very fragrant, hanging in dense clusters or racemes ten to twenty centimetres (four to eight inches) long in June. In the event of a previous warm summer and a following mild spring, the displays of blossom are spectacular. The fruits are pea-like brown pods, five to ten centimetres (two to four inches) in length, hanging in dense clusters into the winter. Locust Trees multiply vigorously by sucker growth away from the parent tree.

Norway Maple
Acer platanoides

A native throughout most of Europe, the Norway Maple was introduced to Britain in the 1600s. It is thought to have just failed to qualify as a native, having narrowly missed crossing by the last land connection from the Continent, about 7500 years ago. It is deservedly a popular decorative tree by virtue of its profuse displays of early pale yellow blossom, its bright green foliage in summer, and magnificent autumn colours. Now it occurs widely in suburbia, parks, woodland plantings, and in gardens of all sizes. Being vigorously self-seeding and able to thrive on almost any soil, it has widely established itself as a wild species in southern England. It also occurs, mainly as a garden, park or street tree, as far north as Argyll and Perthshire.

The crown is broadly domed and dense, and bright green in summer. The main branches are spreading, often from a short trunk. The tallest trees can exceed thirty metres (100ft) in height. The bark is pale grey and smooth and finely folded or superficially cracked into fine criss-cross ridges. The leaves unfold in April, a delicate green tinged with ephemeral pink, crimson or russet. By May they have become completely fresh light green with paler undersides. In autumn they turn butter yellow or gold and, less frequently, scarlet or orange. In shape they are broad and five-lobed, the paired base lobes being roughly triangular. The top and opposing side lobes are sharply shouldered and almost parallel-sided. The tips and shoulders of each lobe are extended into long, filamentous points, and similar lesser points occur sparingly around the leaf, which can be up to fifteen centimetres (six inches) long. The petioles or stalks are long, pale green and milky when crushed.

The yellow or yellow-green flowers open in March, before the leaves, in clusters of thirty to forty, grouped into minor clusters on short, more or less erect panicles. There may be flowers of one or both sexes on one inflorescence, and, less commonly, all flowers are perfect (that is, with stamens, ovaries and surrounding petals or sepals within the same flower). The seeds or 'keys' are green or yellow-green, sometimes tinged with red, and turn brown in autumn. The spreading wings are almost in line with each other.

There are many cultivars planted in parks, the most frequent being the 'Crimson King' with ruby red leaves, and the 'Schwedleri' variety with deep green-black summer leaves and crimson and orange leaves in autumn.

Sycamore
Acer pseudoplatanus

The Sycamore's native range extends across the mountainous country of central Europe eastwards to the Caucasus. It was possibly introduced originally into Britain by the Romans, but more important further introductions took place in the fifteenth century. By the seventeenth century it had become a prestige ornamental tree. Nowadays it is common everywhere, as far north as the Scottish Isles. It is found in town and country parks, gardens, lining streets, and is sometimes grown as a windbreak to exposed farm dwellings, and to provide shelter from sea winds. It has naturalized itself so efficiently, by its prolific seeding and high germination rate, that it is commonly mistaken for a native tree. It colonizes wasteland, cleared woods, abandoned quarries and neglected commons, in some areas forming pure woods, often competing successfully with the native trees.

In the open, the trees are spreading and roundly domed, often broader than high, with long ascending upper branches, and level to descending lower branches. However, in closed stands or plantations, the trunks are usually straight and clean up to the high canopy. There are trees attaining thirty-five metres (115ft) in height, and they can live to more than 400 years. The bark is smooth and light grey on a muscular looking trunk, cracking in due course into small irregular firm plates, sometimes raised at the edges.

The buds are dark reddish in April-May. The leaves first unfold to orange, brown or reddish. Then they turn to their final matt dark green with pale blue-green undersides, so giving the tree its sombre

OPPOSITE:
Norway Maple *Acer platanoides*

LEFT:
Sycamore *Acer pseudoplatanus*

green appearance and subdued scintillating effect in the wind. The leaves are broad and leathery with five pointed lobes, coarsely and irregularly serrated on the margins. They are ten to twenty-six centimetres (four to ten and a half inches) in length. The petioles or stalks are usually red, but pinkish or yellow in some older trees.

The small, pale yellow flowers grow in racemes of up to fifty pairs on short stalks along a pendulous common stem. The fruits are paired seeds joined together, each enveloped in the base of a long membranous wing or 'key', set at about ninety degrees to the other. They are green, often tinged with red, and turn brown by autumn, when they fall and drift spirally to the ground.

There are varieties and cultivars, one 'Atropurpurea' with leaves of purplish-scarlet undersides, and another, 'Brilliantissima', a smallish tree with a mop-like shape and leaves that go through a spectacular series of colour changes.

Horse Chestnut *Aesculus hippocastanum*

Horse Chestnut
Aesculus hippocastanum

Although a traditional tree of the English countryside, the Horse Chestnut is nevertheless an introduction from the Balkans, arriving in Britain in about 1616. Today it is a very common amenity tree in parks, suburbia and villages, and is widespread in the countryside of England and Wales, but less common in Scotland and Ireland.

Fully grown trees may attain thirty metres (100ft) or more in height and up to 300 years in age. Usually they are widely domed with a dense canopy sweeping nearly to the ground. The bark is smooth and dark grey or reddish-brown, and later flakes into scales, lifting at the edges. The twigs are distinctive with their horseshoe-shaped leaf-scars, girdle-scars left by terminal bud scales of previous years, and the short dark reddish-brown terminal buds sticky with resin.

The stalkless leaves are palmate, fanning out from a common centre like the fingers of a hand at the end of a stout yellow-green stem. They are narrow at the base and broader near their ends, which culminate in a point. The longest measure up to twenty-five centimetres (ten inches). The colour is fresh green in May but later becomes darker, and the undersides of the leaves are pale yellow or bluish-green. Autumn leaves are golden, orange or, less frequently, scarlet.

The Horse Chestnut germinates very readily to produce young saplings, but most of these are either overwhelmed by the native vegetation or are eaten by livestock. A few do survive to become mature wild trees on good, rich soils.

The white five-petalled flowers have yellow centres which attract pollinating insects. After pollination, the centres become red. They are arranged in erect, pyramidal panicles or 'candles' of about fifty to sixty flowers, usually densely grouped in fives on short stalks, radiating from the common central stem. The fruits are the well-known shiny, reddish-brown 'conkers' encased, before release, in a green, spherical, two-valved capsule armed with flexible spikes. When they burst open, one shiny spherical conker or two to three smaller nuts, flattened on one side, are revealed.

4: INTRODUCED TREES

There are at least 600 species of tree now growing in Britain, with varying degrees of hardiness, some needing attention and protection from our climate and from competing native vegetation. Only thirty-three to thirty-nine of these 600 species are native. The following descriptions form a selection of the most well known and hardy of the over 550 introduced trees.

Ginkgo or Maidenhair
Ginkgo biloba

Although a broadleaved deciduous tree, the Ginkgo is the most primitive tree living today, apart from cycads and tree ferns. The sperms need to swim in a film of moisture before they can fertilize the female ovule. It is the only surviving species of a primitive order of trees which dominated the flora of the world some 200,000,000 years ago, before all but the most primitive conifers had evolved.

The Ginkgo is now rare as a wild tree, found only in the forests of Chekiang Province in China. Before it was first planted in England, at Kew in 1761, it had for centuries been cultivated in Chinese monasteries and in Japan. Today it is planted along streets and in parks and gardens throughout the world. In Britain it grows best in southern England. It can attain a height of twenty-eight metres (ninety-two feet), and may live to 250 years.

The tree may be narrow in shape, and raggedly and acutely conical. Some specimens have one or more branches extending horizontally far beyond the general outline of the tree. Others are fuller, particularly towards the bottom of the crown, and narrow markedly towards the top. The bark is rough, brownish or dull grey, and deeply fissured.

The leaves are the Ginkgo's most recognizable feature. They are bi-lobed and fan-shaped, without a central midrib and with the veining itself fan-like. The shoots are short, dark, segmented and peg-like. The clusters of leaves originate from them on long stalks. Male and female flowers

Ginkgo or Maidenhair
Ginkgo biloba

Monkey-puzzle or Chile
Pine *Araucaria araucana*

are on separate trees, the flowers appearing on the shoots. The fruits are green and plum-like. They become a malodorous, pulpy mess below in autumn, and for this reason not many female trees are planted. They rarely flower or produce fruit in Britain.

Monkey-puzzle Tree or Chile Pine
Araucaria araucana

The Monkey-puzzle Tree is a member of a primitive genus of evergreen conifers, the *Araucaria*. This had a worldwide distribution up till Cretaceous times (65–70,000,000 years ago), but is now restricted to the southern hemisphere. The natural range of the Monkey-puzzle Tree is now on both sides of the Andes of Chile and Argentina. It was first planted at Kew in 1795 as saplings, which had been raised by Archibald Menzies during his return voyage from Chile as a member of the Vancouver Expedition to the Pacific coast of North America. The main plantings were made when, in 1844, William Lobb sent home large quantities of seeds. From then on it was planted in gardens and parks in Britain and Ireland as a novel ornamental tree. It is the only species of *Araucaria* which can thrive in Britain. The best specimens grow in the west and north west, where they find the cool, moist conditions, without too much frost, approximating their native habitat on the flanks of the Andes.

Its scaly, armadillo-like foliage distinguishes this tree from any other in Britain. It has a regular rounded dome, with a crown that can be either narrow or broad. The crown can extend right to the base of the tree in ideal conditions, but competition from other trees, especially in close stands, and a drier and frostier climate, for example in the eastern half of Britain, kill off the lower branches. Some trees are very lofty, up to thirty metres (100ft) and 150 years is a good age for the Monkey-puzzle Tree.

The branches grow in regular whorls, the upper ones ascending, the middle ones level and arching upwards at the ends, and the lower ones descending to drooping. The bark is dark grey and ringed with fine furrowed bands, with wider light grey bands occurring at regular intervals up the trunk. This pattern is broken by many oval branch scars.

The spiny leaves are three to four centimetres (about one and a half inches) long and, on vigorous trees, cover the branches to the trunk. They are spear-shaped and slightly concave above, and extremely tough and leathery, with a sharp point. A dark glossy green with yellow margins and tips, they surround the shoot, completely cladding it. They point either vertically or slightly forward.

The male and female flowers are usually, though not invariably, on separate trees. The male flowers are in clusters of up to six pointed, ovoid cones of brown, sharp-tipped scales about ten centimetres (four inches) long, which shed their pollen in June. The female flowers are solitary and terminal on the ends of shoots. They take two years to mature into erect, sharply spined, green to golden spheres. They are about fifteen centimetres (six inches) across and are to be found on the upper sides of shoots at the top of the tree. They break up to release the seeds while still on the tree. The seeds are bright brown and edible.

Lawson's Cypress
Chamaecyparis lawsoniana

Lawson's Cypress is native to north-west California and Oregon, where it is now reduced to only a few wild stands. However, as a planted tree it is ubiquitous. It was first introduced into Britain by Lawson's Nurseries in Edinburgh in 1854. It is probably the most widely planted tree in Britain, occurring in parks, churchyards, gardens and arboreta, as well as being planted as shelter-belts. Plantings in Europe are very subject to genetic variations, and many of these have been exploited to produce the numerous varieties of cultivars now on the market. These range attractively in colour from blue to green and yellow, and vary in leaf form.

The typical shape is narrow and regularly conical with the branch ends turned up, and the leading shoot on the apex of the tree, drooping. Single stems are usual, but double or multi-boled trees occur. The tallest trees exceed thirty-five metres (115ft) in height. The bark is smooth and brownish-green, becoming purplish-

Lawson's Cypress
Chamaecyparis lawsoniana

Coast Redwood *Sequoia sempervirens*

brown and fissured into long, vertical plates, flaking away at the ends in old trees.

In this type of tree, the foliage is arranged in opposite pairs on the stem, and is scale-like, in flattened fern-like sprays. The leaves closely enclose the shoots in a series of jointed segments with free tips. There is a translucent gland on the upper and lower leaves which emits a resinous parsley-like scent when crushed. The typical leaf colour is dark green above and paler beneath.

The male flowers are minute, crimson, club-shaped droplets on the ends of shoots, and the globular, scaled, pea-like female cones are set further back on short stalks along the shoots. They are woody when ripe after having released the winged seeds.

Coast Redwood
Sequoia sempervirens

The native distribution of the Coast Redwood is now confined to a narrow strip running parallel to the Californian coast. Here the trees grow close together in stands, so that the trunks tower branchless up to sixty metres (200ft) or more. They are the tallest trees in the world, the highest specimen being nearly 120 metres (400ft) high, and more than 2000 years old. Introduced into Britain via St Petersburg in 1843, it is now frequent as an ornamental tree in parks, gardens and country estates.

It prefers moist conditions and does not tolerate too much frost, and is therefore taller and healthier in western Britain and Perthshire in Scotland, where they are still growing. The tallest tree, over forty-eight metres (160ft) high, is at Bodnant Gardens, near Conwy in Wales. Further east they are frequently scorched by the frost.

When young, it is an open conical tree with a point, the branches arranged in whorls. In more mature trees, the crown thickens and becomes slender and columnar. In older trees it thins out and usually loses its top. The branches are long and downward sloping. The bark is rufous red at first, becoming a darker reddish-brown and deeply fissured in older trees, and is always soft and stringy.

The young foliage has feathery side and

terminal shoots, with two flat rows of hard, sharp-pointed, linear leaves. The young leaves are a fresh light green, the older leaves a darker green. All are whitish-green on the underside, with a fine dark green midline. The major branchlets are more thinly covered with dark green, forward pointing, awl-shaped leaves.

The male flowers are pale yellow and brown 'droplets', about three millimetres (one eighth of an inch) long, on the very tips of the finest shoots. They release their pollen in February. The female flowers are also found at the tips of side shoots. They are globular to egg-shaped, with wrinkled scales which become woody and open out upon seeding to reveal their attachment to a central column.

Giant Sequoia, Wellingtonia or Sierra Redwood
Sequoiadendron giganteum

The Giant Sequoia is now confined as a native tree to groves on the western flanks of the Sierra Nevada mountains of California, where it once formed extensive forests. If not the tallest, it is certainly the most massive tree in the world. The tallest individual, the 'General Grant', is ninety metres (295ft) high. It lives to a great age, the oldest being over 3000 years old.

The first seed was sent to Britain in 1853, to Errol near Perth and to Veitch's Nursery at Exeter. Soon more seed was being planted on almost every large estate throughout Britain. Many of these trees are still growing, the tallest recorded being some fifty metres (165ft) high. It now occurs everywhere as a specimen and ornamental tree in arboreta, parks, cemeteries, avenues and, occasionally, in woods and copses.

The crown is narrow and conical, with a pointed or rounded top. It towers over the surrounding trees. Its upper branches are ascending, the middle ones level, and the lower ones steeply descending. All arch upwards at their extremities. The trunk tapers rapidly upwards from the base of most trees, before becoming almost cylindrical, with only a slight taper. It extends to the very top of the tree. The base is often fluted. The bark is very thick, soft, yielding and fibrous and ranges from an orange to a dark reddish-brown. In

Giant Sequoia, Wellingtonia, Sierra Redwood, Big Tree, or Mammoth Tree
Sequoiadendron giganteum

Japanese Red Cedar
Cryptomeria japonica

mature trees it becomes split with deep, long vertical cracks.

The branchlets are slim, hard cords sheathed in small, dark green scale leaves which are pressed closely to the stem, but with the tips free and slightly spreading. The sprays are upright at the ends of the shoots. They emit an aroma of aniseed when crushed.

The male flowers are minute white droplets borne in dense clusters on the ends of the shoots. They turn yellow when they are ready to release their pollen in March-April. The female cones are egg-shaped, five to eight centimetres (two to three inches) long, and attached to drooping stalks at the ends of the branches, often in dense clusters. They are green at first, and then turn brown as the scales open after two years. The scale-ends are flat and diamond-shaped, with wrinkles radiating from a central fold. They are attached to a stout central stem.

Japanese Red Cedar
Cryptomeria japonica

The Japanese Red Cedar is the redwood of Japan and China, each region having its local forms. It is the principal large forest and plantation tree of Japan. Introduced to Britain from China in 1841, a further introduction took place from Japan in 1861. Specimen trees are now locally frequent in arboreta and country estates, while they are less common in town parks and private gardens. It grows more luxuriantly in the west, the tallest individuals, some forty metres (130ft) high, being located at Endsleigh, near Tavistock.

The crown is tall and conical with a rounded top, and the bright green foliage grows in patches or minor crowns. The lower branches frequently descend steeply to touch the ground before curving upwards, and layering is known to take place to produce new trees. The peripheral branchlets are slender and pendulous, densely clad by the sharp, forward pointing awl-shaped leaves, which are arranged in five vertical rows. The orange to red-brown bark is thick, soft and stringy and, in older trees, peels in strips.

The yellow male flowers are profuse and situated at the end of the finest shoots, and release their pollen in March-April. The green rosette-like female flowers are

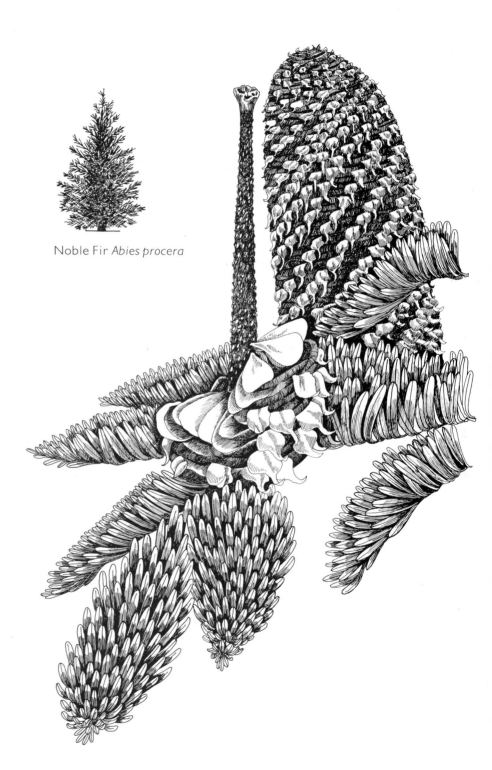

also terminal on the major shoots. The globular cones turn woody after shedding their seed. Each scale bears a triangular flap pointing towards the base, and five or six minor spines pointing in the opposite direction.

Noble Fir
Abies procera

The Noble Fir is a native forest tree of the Cascade Mountains of California and Oregon. Seeds were sent to Britain by David Douglas in 1830, and more trees were planted in 1870 to replace the diseased European Silver Firs. They thrive in western Britain, and do particularly well in north-east Scotland, attaining heights of forty-five metres (148ft) or more. They are common as ornamental and landscaping trees in parks and large gardens, and are also planted commercially.

Initially the tree is narrowly conical, but broadens out in maturity, older trees becoming level-topped and columnar. In young trees the crowns are very dense and the branches are level and arranged in regular whorls. Lower down, the branches become flatter. The bark is silvery-grey or dark purple with shallow cracks. More widely dispersed, deeper cracking appears on old trees.

The leaves are deep green, greyish green or bluish white. They are flattened with blunt, round tips, and are grooved on top. There are two greyish-white stomatal bands on each side. The branchlets are parted below, and the leaves are densely arranged in opposed rows laterally and above. They completely hide the stem, and are arched upwards and inwards. In the upper crown the foliage is extremely dense and bushy, covering the branches and extending even to the trunk.

The small, globular male flowers are crimson before shedding their pollen in May. The mature female cones are immense in September-October, up to twenty-five centimetres (ten inches) long, and crowd the tops of the upper branches, the cones on the ends causing branches to sag. They display prominent, pointed bract scales, at which stage the seed scales are extremely loosely packed. They peel off during the slightest breeze or vibration. Then, complete with bract scale and

Noble Fir *Abies procera*

Cedar of Lebanon *Cedrus libani*

two seeds, each with a triangular wing, they detach and spiral to the ground. This mode of seed shedding is common to all firs.

Cedar of Lebanon
Cedrus libani

Native to Anatolia, Syria and the Lebanon, the wild stand on Mt Lebanon is a remnant of a once extensive Lebanese cedar forest. It was first introduced into Britain in 1632. Many trees were raised from seed by John Evelyn from 1679. Now many magnificent specimens enhance the landscape on country estates, in parks and large gardens everywhere, the tallest exceeding heights of forty metres (130ft).

Young trees are gaunt and conical with horizontal new shoots, but in open-grown older trees, massive branches arise from a short lower trunk and level out, occasionally arching downwards to touch the ground. The upper part of the trunk typically divides into lofty, vertical limbs, which level off in the canopy to give many trees their flat-topped appearance. Other trees arch gracefully, having, as a result, a broadly domed upper crown. Initially the bark is dark grey and smooth, but soon cracks into fine, irregular rectangles. Upon this, in the older trees, is superimposed a deeper, more widely spaced cracking, confined mainly to the main trunk.

The trees are noted for the layered, tier-like masses of foliage on the horizontal branches. On some trees all layers are parallel. The leaves of the new terminal shoots are single and relaxed, and those of the spur-shoots of the older wood are arranged in rosettes of ten to twenty slightly stiff needles, two to three centimetres (approximately one inch) long.

The male flowers are tapered, granular-looking cylinders. When ripe in October they are about four to five centimetres (one and a half to two inches) long. They grow from the many rosettes of leaves on the upper surfaces of the branchlets. They are pale grey-green, and turn pinkish-brown towards October. The female cones are barrel-shaped and lumpy with a slight hollow or blunt point at the apex. Their general colour when ripe is brown, with purple-tinged upper scale-edges that are wide and level. Seven to fifteen centimetres (three to six inches) long, they are usually sticky with white resin.

Norway Spruce
Picea abies

The commonest of the three spruces that survived the Ice Ages in Europe, the Norway Spruce forms forests on the mountainsides of central Europe and Scandinavia, its range extending into northern Russia. It was eliminated in Britain by the glaciations, and was the first spruce to be reintroduced in the 1500s. Today it features in the landscape as a shelter-belt, pheasant covert and plantation tree, and as an ornamental tree in gardens. There are many unusual dwarf forms in cultivation. It is more frost resistant than the Sitka Spruce and so is planted for preference on the eastern side of Britain. It is the true traditional Christmas tree.

It is a sharp-pointed conical tree with the branches arranged irregularly in whorls, the upper branches ascending steeply towards the leading shoot at the top. In mature trees, which may attain a height of forty metres (130ft), the lower branches are level, but arch upwards towards their extremities. The bark is coppery brown when young, on older trees dark purple broken into round plates.

Most have a 'brush' form of foliage with the shoots spreading in all directions from the branches. A 'comb' form may occur, with the shoots hanging in lines from the more evenly spaced branches, possibly an adaptation against excessive lodgement of snow. There is also a narrow spire-like form from Sweden, another adaptation against heavy snowfall. The leaves are hard, pointed and square in section.

The male flowers are small crimson globes in May. The females are dark red and erect on the ends of the shoots, but become pendulous as they develop into slim, cylindrical, brown cones, measuring twelve to fifteen centimetres (five to six inches) long.

Western Hemlock
Tsuga heterophylla

The Hemlock is to be found growing naturally in Asia and North America. The Western Hemlock is the largest of the

Norway Spruce *Picea abies*

Western Hemlock *Tsuga heterophylla*

species, originating in southern Alaska, western Canada, and northern California, where the trees often exceed sixty metres (200ft). Introduced into Britain in 1851, and common in Scotland, it is a beautiful conifer and adorns many large gardens and parks in England.

The crown has a narrow conical form, often full at the base before tapering towards the pointed top, which invariably terminates in a drooping leading shoot. The branches arch downwards gracefully at their extremities. The bark of the juvenile tree is purple-brown, cracking into flakes. In older trees the bark becomes a darker purple-brown or, occasionally, greyish, with thin clefts merging into irregular ridges.

The leaves are flattened aromatic needles of varying lengths in two irregular rows on both sides of the shoot. They are shiny green above, and have two white bands on the lower surface. They are five to fifteen millimetres (a quarter to three-quarters of an inch) long and have rounded tips. The tiny globular male flowers are red initially, but turn to white-yellow as the pollen is shed. Usually the ovoid female cones hang numerously on small shoots all over the tree. They have soft, rounded scales which are initially green or plum-purple, eventually turning brown by the time the scales open. They measure two to three centimetres (one to one and a quarter inches) long.

Douglas Fir
Pseudotsuga menziesii

One of the tallest trees of the forests which range from north to south of the Pacific Coast of North America, from British Columbia to Mexico, they can attain a height of ninety metres (295ft). They were discovered by Archibald Menzies on Vancouver Island in 1793, and he sent the foliage to Kew Gardens for describing. It was not until 1827 that the first seeds were sent home by David Douglas. These seeds were eagerly reared and planted as ornamental trees by the large estate owners of the day. Later it was discovered that the trees were very fast growing and produced high quality wood. Now it occurs almost everywhere as an ornamental or specimen tree in arboreta, large gardens and as plantations in forestry schemes. They prefer clean air and good, moist, but well drained soil on sheltered valley sides in mountain and hill country. In Britain they seldom exceed a height of sixty-five metres (215ft).

Young trees are conical and sharp pointed in form, usually with ascending branches, but older trees are typically straight and slender with descending branches, upcurved at their extremities. The lowest branches often sweep low to rest on the ground. The young bark is grey-green and resin blistered. The older bark is dark purple and vertically cracked and, as the trees age, the bark becomes thick and corky and pale grey or grey-brown in colour, with deeply split fissures. The leaves are yellow or dark green with two variable white bands underneath, and are two to three centimetres (one to one and a quarter inches) in length. They are flat and needle-like with rounded tips and are spread obliquely sideways in two or three opposite rows along the stem of the shoot or branchlet.

The male flowers are on the terminal ends of new shoots and they release their pollen towards the end of March and in April. The female flowers appear singly or in whorls of two or three on the old shoots. The cylindrical ovoid female cones hang profusely under the outer branchlets at all levels of the tree and are five to eight centimetres (two to three inches) in length. Initially the rounded scales are green, turning light brown by the autumn. The cones are distinguished by papery, three-clefted bract scales that protrude between the seed scales. There is a southern form called the Colorado Douglas Fir *Pseudotsuga menziesii* var. *glauca*.

Corsican Pine
Pinus nigra var. *maritima*

A geographical version of the Black Pine, the Corsican Pine's natural range extends from Corsica to southern Italy and Sicily. It was introduced into Britain in 1792, and is now a valuable commercial plantation tree, particularly on the sandy heaths of southern England and Norfolk, and on sandy coastal wastes. It is also planted widely as a shelter-belt tree, and is common in parks and gardens.

In young trees the crown is narrow, regularly conical and open. The branches

Douglas Fir *Pseudotsuga menziesii*

Corsican Pine *Pinus nigra*
var. *maritima*

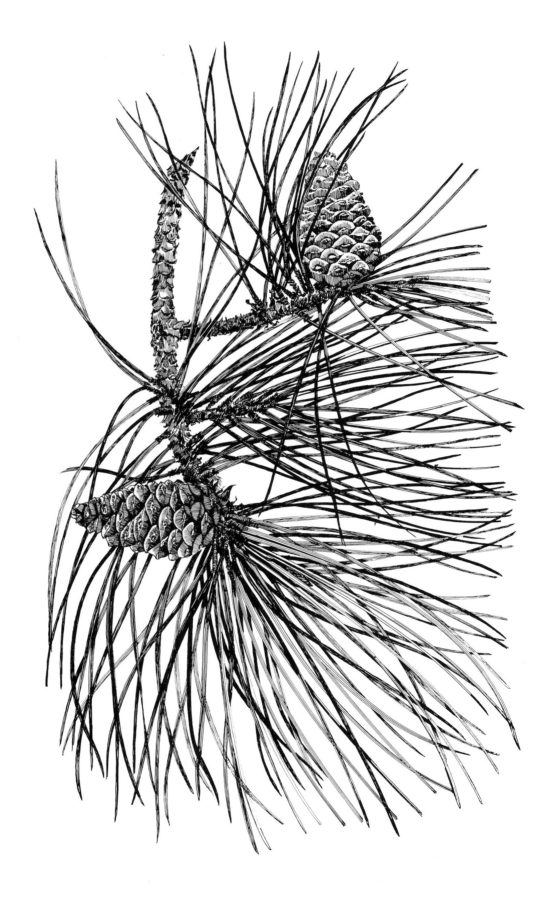

are small, level and well spaced. Old trees become more spreading with longer massive branches, but the single main axis is usually maintained. A fully grown tree can reach more than thirty-five metres (115ft) in height. The bark is usually light or dark grey, but can be pinkish-grey. It is shallowly cracked into long vertical plates, on older trees becoming more deeply cracked into grey plates, often with patches of yellow or light ochre.

The new shoots are slightly ridged, and the buds are brown and squat, terminating abruptly in a fine point. The needles are slender and loose, twelve to eighteen centimetres (five to seven inches) long, growing in pairs from thin, dark brownish-black, scaly sheaths. There is a dark, brownish-black fuzz of disintegrating scales at the bases of the leaves, where they are closely bunched. They are sage or greyish-green, and twisted in young trees.

The male cones are barrel-shaped – short, cylindrical catkins clustered in a circle near the ends of short side shoots, below the terminal bud. They are pale, yellowish-green and speckled, with dark purple stamens. The female flowers are rosy-pink, five millimetres (quarter of an inch) long, and grow singly or in whorls around the terminal buds of new shoots. The cones are long, pointed, egg-shaped and five to eight centimetres (two to three inches) long. They are yellow-brown before turning grey-brown. The scale-ends are somewhat protruding and roughly diamond-shaped, often with the lower margins forming a curve. They are laterally ridged, with a short, blunt prickle surmounting a diamond-shaped umbo, which may be shiny brown or grey. They grow in ones, twos and in whorls of up to four. When the scales open to release the winged seeds, the cones lose their pointed shape.

Monterey Pine
Pinus radiata

The Monterey Pine is a native of limited distribution on the hills around Monterey Bay in California. Elsewhere, it thrives as a fast-growing and vigorous tree, and is planted in many parts of the world as a commercial crop. It was first introduced into Britain in 1833, and now it is widespread as a shelter-belt and ornamental

Monterey Pine *Pinus radiata*

Bristlecone Pine *Pinus aristata*

tree in parks, large country gardens and estates. It has a preference for the milder climates of Ireland and southern and western Britain, though it is found northwards as far as Wester Ross.

Young trees are pointedly conical with ascending branches but, in maturity, they become broadly and irregularly domed or flat-topped trees with stout branches. In old age, the lower branches droop and may touch the ground, and many break off leaving jagged stumps, particularly in closed stands. Heights of up to forty metres (130ft) are attained. The bark is dark brown or grey and becomes deeply fissured.

The needles are bright green, triangular in section, ten to fifteen centimetres (four to six inches) long, and grow in bundles of three, which turn orange-brown before falling after about three years. The small male flowers cluster round the base of the new shoots, and turn yellow in March-April during pollination. The purple female flowers are more sparingly distributed and are clustered round the bases of other shoots.

The ripe cones are squat and ovoid, bluntly pointed, and very asymmetrical at the base, where they are attached to the branch by extremely short hidden stalks. They point backwards towards the base of the tree and are clustered in whorls of three to five. Initially they are green and turn yellowish or orange-brown by the third year, with prominent shiny, rounded scale ends, tipped with rounded knobs. They persist on the branches for up to forty years, eventually turning very woody and dark grey. In nature the heat of a forest fire is needed before the scales open out to release the seeds. The weight of massive clusters of cones sometimes cause branches to break off in very old trees.

Bristlecone Pine
Pinus aristata

Bristlecone Pines are to be found on the bare and desolate slopes of the Rockies, in Colorado, California, Nevada and Utah, and there are small areas in Arizona and New Mexico. It was assumed that all Bristlecone Pines belonged to the single species *Pinus aristata*. However, Dr Dana Bailey has established that the Colorado

Bristlecones are decidedly different from those of Utah, California and Nevada, and has renamed the latter group *Pinus longaeva*. The Bristlecone Pine was first cultivated in Britain in 1863, but is still rare in collections, which include Kew, Wisley and the Royal Botanic Gardens, Edinburgh.

The Bristlecone Pines are the oldest living trees on Earth. Ring counts, of specimens which have been cut down, have revealed ages in excess of 4800 years. Hence the often quoted age of 5000 years is a possibility. They have a narrow, irregularly conical form with some up-swept projecting branches. In Britain they have attained ten metres (thirty-three feet) in height so far. The bark is grey to black, and smooth.

The leaves are in bundles of five, crowded and forward pointing, and closely pressed to an orange shoot. They are two to four centimetres (one to one and a half inches) long, harsh, stiff and abruptly short-spined. They are often called 'foxtails'. They are dark green with occasional white resin spots and are bluish-white on the inner surface. The cones are five to six centimetres (two to two and a half inches) long, ovoid and dull purple with brown spines spreading at right angles from the scales.

Bhutan Pine
Pinus wallichiana

Native to a range extending from Afghanistan to Nepal, the Bhutan Pine was introduced into Britain in 1835. Today it is generally common in gardens, country parkland and urban parks. When young it is a conical tree with an open crown and regularly whorled branches, but it matures into a broader tree with heavy branches. The lower branches droop and often sweep to the ground, bringing within reach some of the long, cylindrical, banana-shaped cones. Trees may attain a height of thirty-five to forty metres (115–130ft). The bark is orange or pinkish-brown and shallowly cracked into narrow vertical plates.

The mature needles are triangular in section, and are long and slender, very loose and flexible, and inclined to be pendulous. They arise in bundles of five from basal sheaths. The outer surfaces are

Bhutan Pine *Pinus wallichiana*

Lombardy Poplar *Populus nigra* var. *'Italica'*

green, and the inner bluish white. The new shoots are hairless and smooth, and bloomed blue-grey. The buds are cylindrical, orange and grey, and often pointed.

The small male flowers are densely grouped at the bases of young shoots or at intervals on longer ones, and become yellow when they release their pollen in June. The female flowers are inconspicuous club-like cylinders on the tips of shoots. They turn pinkish, and then mature in the second year into long, curved, cylindrical cones, hanging under the branch ends. These cones are twenty to thirty centimetres (eight to twelve inches) long, green or purple and very sticky to the touch. Towards autumn they become brown and woody, and the scales open to release the triangular-winged seeds, two from each scale. Some open while on the tree, and others fall before opening.

Lombardy Poplar
Populus nigra var. *'Italica'*

The Lombardy Poplar is the southern European race of our native Black Poplar *Populus nigra betulifolia*. It is native to northern Italy, and was introduced into Britain in 1758 by Lord Rochford, who planted it at St Osyth's Priory in Essex. Cuttings from this tree were soon growing at a phenomenal rate in most parts of the British Isles. It flourishes especially in the loams of river valleys and plains, where it grows fastest and reaches its greatest heights, and has become a familiar feature of the countryside. It is often planted in rows and avenues, alongside roads, in cemeteries and playing fields.

It has ascending branches, and is an extremely fastigiate form of poplar, with its branches ascending almost vertically. Its crown is narrow and columnar, tapering to a pointed apex, giving the illusion of a greater height than in actuality, though the tallest reach up to forty metres (130ft). They can live up to 150 years. The bole develops buttresses as the tree grows, in many cases sprouting burrs and dense foliage. In young trees the bark is dark grey and flatly shiny, becoming cracked into vertical ridges with age.

Older trees often lose their tops in strong winds and develop several vertical trunks which produce a wider and flatter top, so offering a greater resistance to the wind. This is why the municipal safety practice of pollarding Lombardy Poplars is in fact misguided, succeeding only in increasing the danger of falling branches and trees.

The leaves are smooth, slightly shiny and broad, varying between diamond-shaped and triangular. They measure on average six by four and a half centimetres, (two and a half by one and a half inches), and are broadest nearer to the base than to the acutely pointed apex – a deltoid shape similar to those of our native Black Poplar. The stalks or petioles are pale yellow and flattened, and about two and a half centimetres (one inch) long. The leaf margins are regularly toothed, and their colour is bright green above and paler beneath, turning to yellow in autumn.

The Lombardy Poplar is a male clone and, hence, can reproduce only by suckers or cuttings. It produces crimson catkins similar to, if smaller than, those of our male native Black Poplar.

Caucasian Wingnut
Pterocarya fraxinifolia

A native of the Caucasus and northern Iran, the natural range of the Caucasian Wingnut is the most westerly of the seven species of wingnut. It was introduced into Britain in about 1872. Today it is a rather uncommon ornamental tree in gardens, parks and arboreta, principally in southern England although specimens may be found northwards as far as Edinburgh. It grows best on moist, loamy soils, preferably near water.

The Caucasian Wingnut can be either a wide spreading tree on a short, gnarled trunk, with radiating ascending main branches and level-to-drooping terminal branchlets, or an open complex of sinuous trunks. In either form it can sucker rampantly, producing a dense thicket radiating from the base. The tallest trees have attained about twenty-two metres (seventy-two feet) in height. The bark is a dull grey and brown, with a network of ridges interspersed with knobs and bosses.

The leaves are pinnate, alternately arranged along the branchlets and tending to droop. They consist of a central stem or 'rachis' up to sixty centimetres (two feet)

Caucasian Wingnut
Pterocarya fraxinifolia

long, with three to thirteen pairs of opposed, sessile (stalkless), oblong, pointed leaflets with a single terminal leaflet. The middle leaflets are the longest. Between the pairs of leaflets the rachis is rounded in section. In contrast to other species of wingnut, the rachis of the Chinese Wingnut *Pterocarya stenoptera* is broadly flanged. The rachis between the paired leaflets of the Hybrid Wingnut (a cross between the Caucasian and Chinese Wingnuts) is narrowly flanged or grooved – a characteristic which is intermediate between those present in the parent species. The leaves are bright shiny green above and paler beneath, and turn yellow in the autumn.

Male and female catkins grow on the same tree in all species of wingnut. In April they are slender and pendulous, the female catkins ripening into conspicuous strings of broad-winged nuts. Those of the Chinese Wingnuts are more narrowly winged than those of the Caucasian Wingnuts. Those of the Hybrid Wingnut are more fully winged and densely packed on the stem. The pith of the shoots of all wingnuts is chambered, not solid, a characteristic shared by the closely related walnuts.

Szechuan or Sichuan Birch
Betula platyphylla
var. 'szechuanica'

A native of Szechuan (now Sichuan), a province of south-west China, the Szechuan Birch is a Chinese form of the Far Eastern version of our native Silver Birch. The first seeds planted in Britain were sent by Ernest Wilson in 1908, and the largest trees now living in this country were probably grown from these seeds. Today it is planted widely in many parks and gardens, in both town and country.

Like other birches it is a medium-sized, short-lived pioneering tree, growing up to eighteen metres (sixty feet) in height. It is planted for its almost unblemished milky white bark, which leaves a chalky powder on the hands when touched. The bark peels away in strips. The foliage is light, the leaves being a bright green in early summer. They are large and broadly spear-shaped, with a rounded base which is the widest part of the acutely pointed leaf. The leaf margins are coarsely ser-

Szechuan or Sichuan Birch
Betula platyphylla var.
'szechuanica'

rated and there are six to eight pairs of veins. The leaves are smooth and leathery to the touch, and have translucent spots underneath.

Hungarian Oak
Quercus frainetto

Native to Italy, the Balkans, Hungary and Czechoslovakia, the Hungarian Oak was introduced into Britain in 1838. Many fine specimens can be seen at Osterley Park, West London. It is now common as an ornamental tree in many large gardens and parks.

Probably the most handsome of oaks, its magnificent domed crown is supported by straight branches radiating from a clean cylindrical trunk. The tallest specimens are thirty metres (100ft) or more in height. Many old specimens were grafted onto a base of English Oak, the trunks of such trees being frequently thick with sprouts. The bark is pale grey, sometimes brownish, and is deeply cracked into short, fine ridges.

The leaves are larger than those of most oaks, varying in length from fifteen to twenty-five centimetres (six to ten inches). They are oblong ovate in shape, with the widest part between mid-length and the tip, and are deeply incised into seven to ten lobes. The lobes are often overlapping and floppy. Below the widest point, the leaf tapers gradually to a narrow basal auricle, or ear, each side of the short petiole. They are a rich green above and greyish-green and pubescent (hairy) beneath. Seen from a distance from the tree, the deeply cut leaves can easily be recognized on the edge of the crown, an unmistakeable point of identification.

The female flowers are minute clusters of stalkless pale brown ovals, around the terminal buds. They are tipped with deep purple stigmas. The acorns are about two and a half centimetres (one inch) in length, and are seated in cupules, or cups, with loosely overlapping scales.

Red Oak
Quercus rubra

The Red Oak is one of four species of red oak in America, ranging from eastern North America (including Canada) south to Texas. Introduced into Britain in 1724, it is now commonly planted in parks,

Hungarian Oak *Quercus frainetto*

Red Oak *Quercus rubra*

gardens, arboreta and urban settings throughout Britain. It is also planted to add variety to conifer plantations, and for the variety of its autumn colours, which may be cigar-brown, golden, orange or deep red.

As a juvenile tree it is open crowned and broadly conical, but it soon loses this shape to become broadly domed with straight branches radiating from a short main trunk. Mature trees can attain heights of over thirty metres (100ft). The bark of all trees of the American red oak group is smooth. In this species it is silvery grey or brownish-grey and, as the tree matures, it develops a few fissures, small rough plates occurring on the lower trunks of older specimens.

The leaves are variable in size, averaging twelve to twenty-five centimetres (five to ten inches) in length. The largest, which are generally on strong sprouts or young saplings, can be twenty to thirty centimetres (eight to twelve inches) long. Generally they are ovoid in shape, narrowest at the base, where they are wedge-shaped, and widest at the midpoint or beyond. They are jagged in outline, the leaf being either shallowly or more deeply incised into four or five lobes. Each lobe terminates in a sharp point, with one or more equally acute points on either side. The lobes are at an angle of forty or forty-five degrees, and each half of the leaf may be asymmetrical.

There are four to five pairs of veins, each one terminating at the apex of a lobe and extending beyond it as a fine filament. The petiole is about two centimetres (one inch) long and yellowish or pale green. The new leaves unfurl from the buds in spring a clear bright yellow which persists for two or three weeks or more, before they turn dark, matt green above and pale matt greyish-green beneath. The male catkins are yellow, pendulous filaments. The female flowers are inconspicuous red ovals in the axils of the fresh yellow leaves. Both sexes are on the same tree. The first year's acorns are minute brown spigolos on the second-year branchlets. The ripe acorns mature in the second year, in common with all red oaks, and are quite large, measuring two by two centimetres (one by one inch). They are set in shallow cups.

Caucasian Elm or Zelkova
Zelkova carpinifolia

The Caucasian Elm is closely related to the elms, but is in fact a member of a distinct group of trees. It grows wild in the Caucasian and Elburz mountains, where it takes its normal shape; in Britain, inexplicably, most specimens take the form of a giant egg-shaped crown, with a dense mass of steep and vertical stems arising from a short, thick trunk. Introduced into Britain in 1760, as seed, it occurs today in some parks and gardens, notably in London and Oxford. It usually grows in stands, with long, sometimes sinuous trunks with a few thicker, upcurved branches.

The trunks of the bushy type are markedly fluted, with smooth, greenish-grey or pale buff bark which scales off in places to reveal crumbling patches of orange. The many outer stems fan out abruptly at one level from the trunk at heights varying from one to three metres (three to ten feet) above the ground. When they die, the inner stems rot *in situ* as they are unable to fall. The oldest trees are thirty metres (100ft) or more in height and many trees are 160 years old and still growing.

The leaves are elliptical and pointed with six to twelve pairs of veins and coarse, broad marginal teeth which can be either rounded or pointed. They are arranged alternately on the shoot, and average five to nine centimetres (two to three and a half inches) in length. Dull or shiny green above and downy beneath, they turn orange or brownish-orange in autumn before they fall.

The fruits are not, as in true elms, nuts embedded in membranous discs: they are green, lumpish four-ridged nutlets about five millimetres (quarter of an inch) in length growing at the base of the leaves. However, in Britain they rarely form. The male and female flowers are on the same twig. The Caucasian Elm can sucker freely, and is capable of forming a hedge.

Southern or Bull Bay Magnolia
Magnolia grandiflora

Magnolias are primitive flowering plants and were first introduced into Britain in 1734. The Southern Magnolia is an evergreen, native to North America from

Caucasian Elm *Zelkova carpinifolia*

Southern or Bull Bay Magnolia *Magnolia grandiflora*

North Carolina to Texas. In Britain it is an entirely ornamental tree, commonly grown on the sunny sides of garden walls. It is frequent in gardens, parks and arboreta in the southern parts of Britain and Ireland. It is a broadly conical tree capable of achieving heights of up to fourteen metres (forty-five feet) and the bark is blackish-grey and smooth.

The buds are about fifteen millimetres (three-quarters of an inch) long and greenish-brown with rust-coloured, hairy tips. The thick leathery leaves are long and pointed-elliptical or oblong, the margins without teeth and sometimes wavy. They are a rich glossy green above and matt green beneath with a rust-coloured pubescence. They vary from nine to sixteen centimetres (three and a half to six and a half inches) in length.

The flowers do not blossom simultaneously, as do Asiatic magnolias, but sparingly from July to September. They are erect, fragrant, and cup-shaped when fully open, measuring twenty to twenty-five centimetres (eight to ten inches) across. The six broad white 'petals' are undifferentiated sepals and petals. The fruits are cylindrical cones composed of many purplish-green, hairy scales which are the individual fruits.

Tulip Tree
Liriodendron tulipifera

The Tulip Tree is evolutionarily the most advanced of the magnolia family, but is still a primitive broadleaved tree. It is abundant in the woods and countryside of eastern North America, from where it was introduced into Britain in about 1650. Today it is a common and favourite ornamental tree in gardens, parks and country estates. The largest and most profusely flowering trees are in southern England.

It is a magnificent tree with its dense, tumbling and glossy green foliage, which often obscures the delicate cream-coloured flowers. It can attain a height of thirty-five metres (115ft). The crown on young trees is conical or roughly conical with ascending upper branches. Some older trees are tall and columnar, with domed or flattish tops supported by a straight trunk extending high up into the crown. Other trees may be broader and irregular in shape with several billowing crowns in summer. The bark is grey with a network of ridges. In older trees it turns a pale orange-yellow and can become gnarled. Some trees have reached at least 300 years of age.

The leaves are glossy green above and paler underneath, turning a rich brown or glorious golden yellow in autumn. They are very distinctive in shape, having four lobes and giving a truncated appearance. The inner margins of the top pair of lobes diverge from a central cleft at a very obtuse angle – almost in a straight line – to the pointed, angular upper corners of the leaf. The side lobes give the leaves a slightly winged appearance.

The flowers are 'perfect', each one comprising both male and female parts, They consist of an inner corolla of six 'true' petals and only three pale, greenish-white sepals which are curled backwards in the open flower. The petals are a delicate light green or primrose on the outside, with blotches or zones of orange near the base of the flower. They are white to delicate greenish-white on the inside, with similar orange blotching. The fleshy linear stamens are orange or yellow-orange, and surround the central white-to-greenish cone, which is an aggregate of styles and tipped dark red anthers. The fruits remain on the tree throughout the winter: they are brown, paper-like erect cones, which later disintegrate to release the individual winged seeds.

The Chinese Tulip Tree *Liriodendron chinensis* is a broader tree, and the leaves have narrower side lobes which form a deeper, more pronounced waist where they join the upper lobes. The upper margins of the leaves are almost in a straight line from the central cleft.

Sweet Gum
Liquidambar styraciflua

The Sweet Gum is a member of the Wych Hazel family (*Hamamelidaceae*), with close relatives within its genus in Asia Minor, south-east China and Taiwan. It is an abundant forest tree of eastern North America, ranging southwards from New York State through Mexico to Nicaragua, where it becomes evergreen. Introduced into Britain in 1681, it has been planted in parks, gardens and arboreta, mainly in the southern halves of England, Wales and

Tulip Tree *Liriodendron tulipifera*

Sweet Gum *Liquidambar styraciflua*

Ireland. It is prized chiefly for its magnificent autumn colours.

Young trees have conical or oval-shaped crowns with ascending upper branches. The lower branches are level or drooping, but are typically turned up at the ends. Older trees can be either broadly domed on short trunks or, more frequently, tall-crowned and supported by long, straight trunks. Which form they adopt is probably dependent on whether they grow in the open or in close stands. The tallest trees are about twenty-eight metres (ninety-two feet) high. The bark is light or dark grey or, sometimes, brownish. It is very rough, and is fissured into narrow, vertical, irregular ridges.

The leaves can be mistaken for those of the maples, but they are alternately arranged along the shoot and not in opposed pairs. The middle lobes are typically, but not invariably, much longer than the paired side-lobes, and there are forward-pointing, incurved teeth around the margins.

The leaves of young trees are three- or five-lobed, with the middle lobe usually the longest. They are parallel-sided for most of their length, until the sides curve inwards to meet at the pointed apex. In older trees the leaves are five- or seven-lobed, and often broader in proportion, the lobes being variably rectangular. Length ranges from ten to fifteen centimetres (four to six inches). They unfold in May and are rich shiny green above, and duller beneath. The autumn colours are notably variable – they may be purple, subdued scarlet, bright scarlet, deep red, orange or lemon.

The flowers do not form very often in Britain, the tree being too warmth demanding. The individual flowers are minute. They lack petals and are aggregated into spherical clusters, both sexes being borne on the same tree. The female flowers have two functional ovaries. The fruits hang in green globular clusters from long stalks; they are superficially like those of the plane, but are very spiky.

London Plane
Platanus X hispanica
The London Plane is a hybrid between the Oriental Plane (*P orientalis*) and the American Plane (*P occidentalis*). As its

specific name implies, it traces its origin to Spain. It is a hardy long-living tree, immune from city pollution, which has been extensively planted since the beginning of the twentieth century in the streets of London. It has also been widely planted in southern England and the Midlands in parks and country estates, as well as urban areas, and is less frequent in Ireland and Scotland. The oldest, including giants in Berkeley Square in London, are over 200 years old and still growing. The tallest tree is in Somerset; it is fifty-five metres (180ft) high.

It is a broadly domed tree on a long trunk, and old trees have spreading and often twisting branches. In winter, the twisted and pendulous finer branches and the hanging tassels of female fruits make a pleasing tracery. The bark is smooth, but flakes off in patches to reveal the new yellowish-white underbark, leaving the trunk a dappled combination of grey, brown and yellowish-white. This habit is thought to be accentuated in the London grime, its function to clear the breathing lenticels which become clogged. The bark of old trees becomes orange-brown, with fine vertical fissures and folds, extending high up the trees. There are often burrs on the trunk.

The leaves are similar to those of Norway Maple, but are alternately arranged along the shoot. The bases of the long, red-brown stalks are swollen and hollow, designed to conceal the axillary buds for next year's leaves. They have five trianguloid lobes with coarsely but sharply toothed margins, and the single top lobe may be sharply shouldered. The depth of indentation between the lobes is variable, some being cut by acute sinuses nearer the base than others. Some lobes are broad, nearer to the American Plane, and others are narrower, nearer to the Oriental Plane. The colour is brownish grey-green when the leaves unfold in May, and eventually changes to a fresh, glossy green, paler underneath. Their smoothness repels grime-laden moisture. They are slightly broader than long and measure eleven to twenty-three centimetres (four and a half to nine inches) in length.

Plane trees are wind-pollinated, and the male and female flowers are separately aggregated into globular, tassel-like seed-

London Plane *Platanus X hispanica*

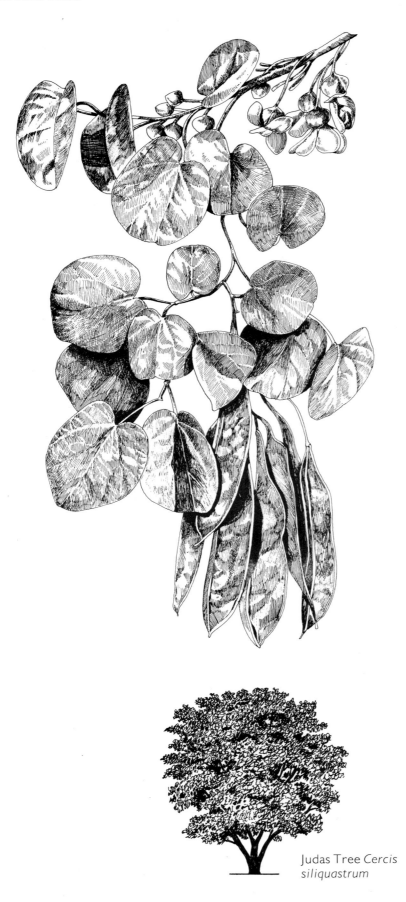

Judas Tree *Cercis siliquastrum*

heads, one to three on long pendulous stalks. The male flowers are yellow prior to releasing their pollen in May. The female flowers are crimson with their protruding anthers. The ripe fruits are four-sided nutlets, tightly packed in hairy down in the pendulous globular fruit clusters.

Judas Tree
Cercis siliquastrum

A member of the pea family, the Judas Tree is a native of the rocky terrain of southern Europe and western Asia. It is grown in parks and gardens as an ornamental tree in southern England and East Anglia. It is a low spreading tree up to twelve metres (forty feet) high, usually on a short main trunk, and often with several small crowns. It usually becomes lopsided in old age, some trees developing upcurving branches which rest on the ground. Initially, the bark is purplish but later becomes dull pink with many fine cracks.

The leaves are nearly circular, and have no teeth on the margins. They are heart-shaped at the base, from which the five main veins radiate. The leaves are dark green or yellowish-green above, and paler or grey-green underneath. They are arranged alternately along the stem on pale green stalks or petioles five centimetres (two inches) long. They resemble the leaves of the Katsura tree, but these are in opposed pairs.

The flowers are bright, rosy pink and pea-like. They are two centimetres (one inch) long, and grow in clusters of three to six on reddish petioles from young shoots, as well as directly from branches and the main trunk. They usually appear before the leaves emerge in May. The fruits are bunches of flat, purplish pods, containing several seeds, becoming brown by autumn and remaining on the tree throughout the winter.

Tree of Heaven
Ailanthus altissima

A member of the Quassia family *Simaroubaceae* of mainly tropical distribution in south-east Asia, the Tree of Heaven was introduced to Britain from northern China in 1751. It is common in the streets, squares and parks of Greater

London, and also in the gardens and parks of southern England and East Anglia. It is infrequent in the north and in Ireland.

The trunk is typically straight and cylindrical for five to six metres (sixteen to twenty feet), and then divides into steeply ascending main branches to form an irregular dome. Fully grown trees can attain a height of twenty-five metres (eighty-two feet). It suckers freely, some suckers sprouting some distance from the trunk. The bark is distinctive, smooth and greyish-brown in young trees, with faint vertical white lines up the trunk. In older trees the bark becomes finely rough and dark grey, with sinuous, pewter-grey or buff streaks.

The leaves are pinnate, arranged in eleven to eighteen opposed pairs of leaflets on a green or red common stem fifteen to thirty centimetres (six to twelve inches) long. The leaflets are on short reddish stalks and are lanceolate, each with an asymmetrical, rounded or angular base with one to three big teeth. Also, they have a crinkled raised glandular patch. They are shiny, deep green above and paler and hairless underneath. They emerge deep red in June and fall green in the early autumn.

The male and female flowers usually appear on separate trees, on panicles, stalked flowers or fruits branching from a central stem. The male flowers are green in June, turning red in July, and later cream when the four short petals of the individual flowers open. The female fruits have one seed centrally placed in flattened and slightly twisted, membranous, oblong wings, which are attractively tinged with red by August. They are grouped in large panicles and drift spirally to earth in autumn.

Smooth Japanese Maple
Acer palmatum

The Smooth Japanese Maple is native to Japan and Korea, and was first introduced as seed by Phillip von Siebald in 1820, when Japan was still a closed country. A favourite ornamental tree in gardens everywhere, it is planted for its varied and striking autumn leaves in both the wild 'type' trees and the many cultivars, some of which maintain their brilliant hues from summer into autumn. The 'type'

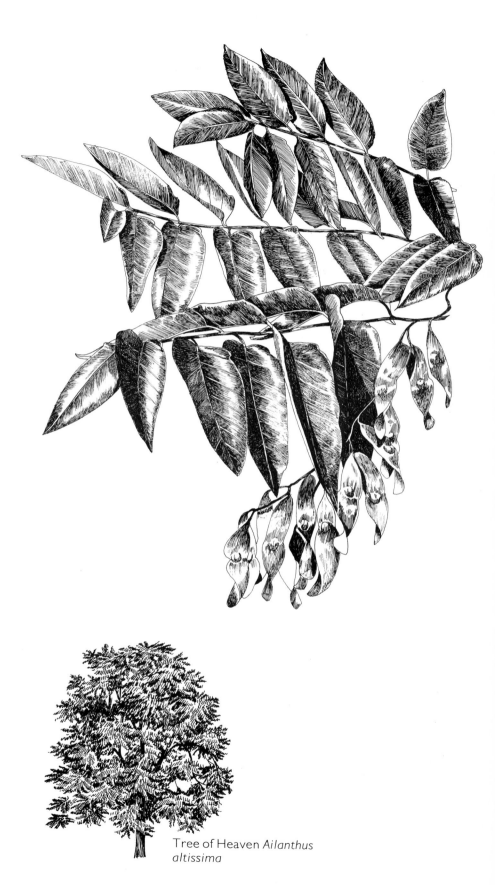

Tree of Heaven *Ailanthus altissima*

99

Smooth Japanese Maple
Acer palmatum

tree is domed and spreading, achieving heights of fifteen metres (fifty feet), but about ten metres (thirty-three feet) is usual. The sinuous trunk divides after a few feet into outwardly curved, ascending main branches, which bear slender, level shoots. Many of the cultivars are bush-size and suitable for small gardens. The bark is smooth, rich brown and striped with pale yellow.

The new shoots are slender and smooth, dark red above and green beneath. The leaf of the wild 'type' tree is bright green, turning to red, crimson or yellow in autumn. It is deeply palmate, divided into five or seven narrow, serrated and spear-shaped lobes, and grows on slender stalks three to five centimetres (one and a quarter to two inches) long.

The flowers are small, dark purple or pink, in erect clusters of twelve to fifteen, on slender green or red stalks. The fruits are erect, pale green winged 'keys', tinged with red, and set at an obtuse angle. Those of most cultivars are pendulous.

There are many cultivars, many of which are low and bushy. The variety 'Atropurpureum' is a common one, growing up to about seven or eight metres (twenty-three to twenty-five feet) high. Its leaves are dark purple and sometimes bright red, with five lobes. Another and rather rare variety is 'Aconita', a straggling tree of bush size with palmate leaves, narrowly cut nearly to the base of the leaf into serrated, narrow, spear-like lobes. They are bright green in summer and turn to a brilliant crimson in autumn. The 'keys' are equally red and difficult to discern against the red leaves.

Silver Pendent Lime
Tilia petiolaris

The Silver Pendent Lime originated in the Caucasus, from a small wild population which is either now extinct, or may continue as a selected variant of the Silver Lime, *Tilia tomentosa*. It is now known only as a garden tree. It was first grown in Britain c 1840, and there are some very tall trees still growing, some as tall as thirty-three metres (108ft) or more. They occur in collections, country parks and gardens.

It does not produce viable seed and must be propagated by grafting onto the base of a large-leafed lime. Two or three erect, sinuous trunks arise from above the graft point, to form a tall, columnar tree with a round or flattish dome, and pendulous outer branches. In summer the crown is very dense and dark green, shimmering silvery-white as the breezes stir the leaves on their long pendulous stems to reveal their undersides. The bark above the graft is dark or pale grey with smooth, shallow ridges.

The leaves are obliquely heart-shaped at the base, broad and rounded-ovate, coming abruptly to a sharp, pointed tip. The margins are serrated with sharp, forward-pointing teeth. The upper surfaces are dark, glossy green and the undersides white and downy. They measure up to twelve by twelve centimetres (five by five inches). They are attached to slender, pendant petioles, which are six to twelve centimetres (two and a half to five inches) in length, and are white and pubescent. In autumn they turn yellow in patches.

The minute, fragrant, yellow flowers of five petals hang in bunches of seven to ten from 'branches' of a common stem, which is attached to a strap-like yellow-green bract. The fruits become hard green 'pellets' eight to ten millimetres (nearly half an inch) long and are slightly warty.

Tupelo
Nyssa sylvatica

Native in woods of the coastal plains of eastern North America and the lower Mississippi Basin, the Tupelo was introduced into Britain before 1750. It is infrequent in large gardens and arboreta in southern England, but many trees were planted at Sheffield Park, Sussex in 1909. It is noted for its vivid autumn colours of scarlet and gold, or mottled cream or pink for trees growing in shady places. The trees grow best on light slightly acid soil in sunny situations.

They are medium-sized trees, measuring about twenty-two metres (seventy-two feet) high when fully grown. They are narrowly or broadly conical trees, with level to down-curved branches, typically curving upwards at the ends. The longest branches are at the base, and the upper ones are ascending to complete a rounded top. The trunk continues nearly to the top of the tree. The bark is fawn or dark grey and coarsely cracked into vertical ridges.

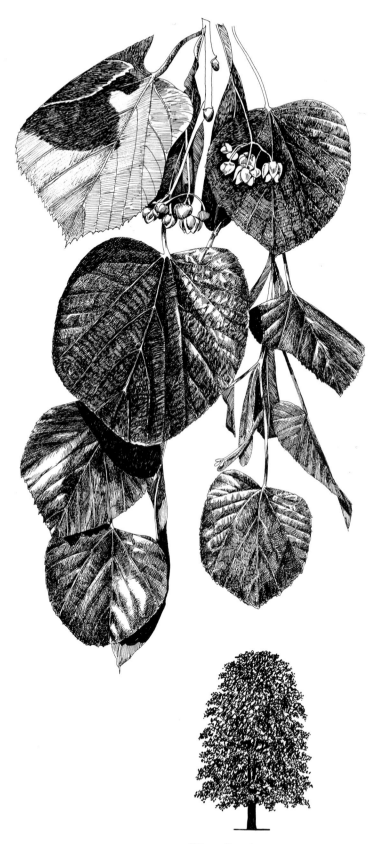

Silver Pendent Lime *Tilia petiolaris*

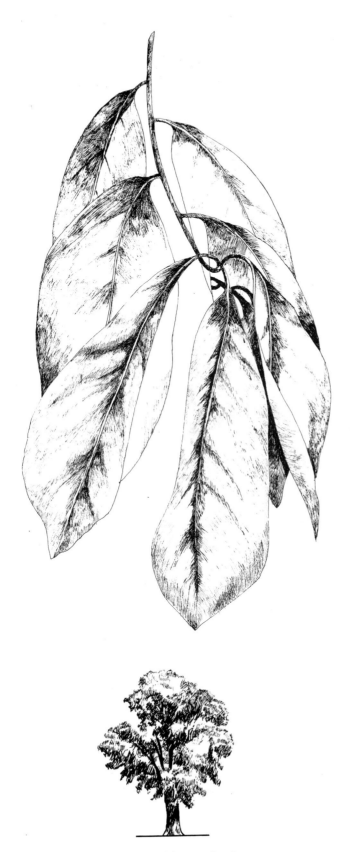

Tupelo *Nyssa sylvatica*

In winter, the shoots are spiky with forward pointing side shoots, which bear the pointed red-brown buds. The leaves are alternate, elliptical and pointed, or roundly obtuse at the tip, narrowing gradually towards the base, where the sides merge with the stem. They measure five to twelve centimetres (two to five inches) long and rarely have marginal teeth; they are glossy and dark or yellow-green above, and whitish-green underneath. The trees have unisexual flowers on the same tree, and the fruits are small, green plum-like drupes, ripening to red or purple.

Dove or Handkerchief Tree
Davidia involucrata

A member of the Tupelo family *Nyssaciaciae*, the Dove Tree is native to central and south-west China. Discovered by Père David in Szechuan (Sichuan) Province in 1869, it was claimed to have been sent to Kew as seed by Ernest Wilson in 1901. However, this was found to be the 'Vilmoriana' variety which had already been sent to Vilmorin's nursery in France in 1897 by Père Fargues. In 1903, Wilson managed to find and send home seeds of the tree described by Père David. It occurs in large gardens and arboreta of southern and western Britain, where it is uncommon, the Vilmorin variety being the more frequent.

It is a conical tree when young, but becomes high domed with radiating branches, the lower ones being level. They all tend to curve downwards towards their extremities. It may attain a height of eighteen to twenty metres (sixty to sixty-five feet). The bark is purple, flaking to expose pale brown or grey-brown underbark, and has fine vertical fissures.

The shoots are dark brown and slightly shiny with pale lenticels, and the buds are ovate and bright shiny red. Visually the leaves are somewhat lime-like, but the five to nine pairs of almost opposed side veins are prominent, and the petioles are pinkish. They are broad, heart-shaped at the base, and long-pointed at the tip. The upper surface is a dull shiny green. A white pubescence, which is absent in the commoner 'Vilmorin' variety, covers the underside. They are up to seventeen centimetres (seven inches) long by fifteen centimetres (six inches) wide (those of the 'Vilmorin' variety being narrower). The margins are serrated with sharp, triangular teeth.

The true flowers emerge with the leaves as globular, purple heads about five millimetres (quarter of an inch) across concealed by two pale yellow bracts. They open out in May into a dense yellow circle of male flowers, each eight millimetres (nearly half an inch) across, with a cylindrical bisexual flower inside. The bracts become white and petal-like, but veined like the leaves, and they hang in pairs like pocket handkerchiefs. The largest of a pair is seventeen centimetres (seven inches) long, hanging from one side, and the other, half its length, hangs from the other. In mass the flowers present an impressive display of white blossom in May and June. The fruits are pear-shaped, three to five centimetres (one and a half to two inches) long, green at first with a purple bloom and buff speckles, later ripening to purple.

Southern Catalpa or Indian Bean Tree
Catalpa bignonioides

A member of the trumpet vine family *Bignoniaceae*, the Indian Bean Tree is native to a coastal belt stretching from Florida to Louisiana, but is now grown throughout the USA. It was introduced to Britain in 1726 by John Catesby. It needs warm summers, and hence grows quicker and flowers more profusely in the southern half of England. Further north it becomes a foliage tree with a very short season, the leaves opening in June-July and falling early.

It is a wide-spreading, domed tree. Its branches usually radiate from a short trunk, and are arched, the lower ones drooping on some trees. Taller trees with longer trunks do occur, and may attain a height of eighteen metres (sixty feet). The bark is often dull pink and brown, scaling off into fine flakes, but can be more grey and cracked into flat ridges.

The new shoots are smooth and greyish-brown with leaf scars. The orange-brown buds are all lateral, terminal buds being absent. The leaves are arranged in whorls of three, usually on

Dove or Handkerchief Tree *Davidia involucrata*

strong shoots, and in opposed pairs. They are large, limp and ovate, with broad, heart-shaped or rounded bases, and are abruptly sharp-pointed at the tip. They grow on long, flat, light green stalks. They are bright green above, and paler and downy underneath, deep purple in young trees. They may measure up to twenty-five centimetres (ten inches) by twenty-two centimetres (eight and a half inches) long, but can be half that length.

The white trumpet-like flowers are densely clustered in panicles, on short stalks attached to a long central stem. The corolla tubes flare out into five petals. They are attractively blotched and spotted with yellow and purple inside. The fruits, fifteen to forty centimetres (six to sixteen inches) long, hang in clusters of slim, dark brown pods from the panicles. They remain on the tree throughout the winter, and later split lengthways into two valves to release the seeds.

Southern Catalpa or Indian Bean Tree *Catalpa bignonioides*

5: THE STATUS OF TREES TODAY: CONSERVATION AND REGENERATION

The natural enemies of trees are stress, caused by the weather and climate, pests, diseases, fire and browsing. Through the ages, trees have been naturally controlled by these forces. Now, however, Man is proving the greatest destroyer of trees and later in this chapter we examine what is happening today and what can be done to reverse this destruction.

THE GREAT STORM

On 16 October 1987, between the hours of four and six am, the storm struck with such awesome power that giant trees weighing several tons were plucked from the soil. The felling of these giants had a 'domino effect' on the immediate under-storey vegetation, which was flattened in its turn.

The storm destroyed many rare tree collections which, in some instances, had taken hundreds of years to cultivate. In particular, the National Trust gardens in Sussex, Surrey and Kent suffered tragically. On entering Nyman's Gardens, near Handcross in Sussex, the scene was reminiscent of those poignant photographs taken after the Battle of Ypres during World War I. The pinetum had disappeared apart from a few topless trunks. Yet, in close proximity, the redwoods were still standing, although some of their top branches had been lost.

Again in Sussex, Wakehurst Place near Ardingly is also a National Trust property. It is an addition to the Royal Botanic Gardens at Kew, and is famous for its heath gardens, rhododendrons and redwoods. The loss of trees like the Pride of India, notable for its conspicuous panicles of yellow flowers and admired by thousands of visitors every year, is incalculable. Many trees were also either felled or badly damaged in the adjacent Bloomers and Bethlehem Woods.

In the Southern Region of the National Parks no less than 320 hectares (798 acres)

of woodland have been totally destroyed, and another 370 hectares (915 acres) badly damaged. In the former category the areas may be allowed to become wildlife refuges or non-intervention areas, so allowing natural regeneration.

The trees' vulnerability to the great force of the wind was increased because they were still in leaf, giving them a sail-like resistance. Furthermore, the ground had been softened by almost continuous rain, and the roots were either too weak or too shallow to hold the trees against the powerful gusts. Falling trees excavated pits as large as one and a half metres (four feet) deep as the plate of roots beneath the trunk swung upwards. As the trees fell, the surface roots dragged a carpet of leaves, litter and woodland herbs with them. Some trees, their roots pulled out of the soil, managed to stay upright by leaning perilously against stronger neighbours, their trunks as taut as bow strings – a chain sawyer's nightmare.

In many cases, notably conifers, the trunks were snapped off well above

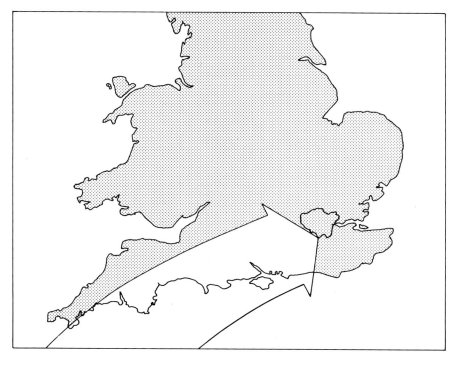

Direction of the path of the storm of October 1987, the greatest storm to strike the south east of Britain since records began. It resulted from a strong depression which intensified quickly over the Bay of Biscay.

ABOVE:
Many of London's familiar trees were destroyed or damaged in their famous parks by the storm, as this one in Hyde Park. The Hilton Hotel, Park Lane, is in the background.

RIGHT:
On the scarp near Colley Hill above Reigate. All the beeches have lost their tops, but the younger supple trees have survived to reach maturity.

ABOVE:
Fallen beeches on
Mickleham Downs, near
Leatherhead, Surrey. Due
to the shallow roots and
the chalk soils, beeches
were plucked effortlessly
from the ground.

LEFT:
Fallen giant beeches,
victims of the storm on
the shallow soils of the
Betchworth Clump, on
the scarp of the North
Downs

Seventeen die as 100mph hurricane blasts across stricken Britain

THE NIGHT WE NEARLY BLEW AWAY

WELL DONE, LADS!

STRANDED: The crippled Sealink ferry, Hengist, high and dry at Folkestone after the hurricane drove her on to a concrete apron stoving in her hull

POWER BLACKOUT CRIPPLES SOUTH

Gales fuse lines

SMASHED: Uprooted trees blown on to homes in Maidstone in the storm

WHY DIDN'T THEY WARN US?

Pictures: ROGER ALLEN, PAUL AMOS and IAN CAMPBELL

ROBERT HEAD, SHEREE DODD and SIMON FERRARI

SMASHED TO BITS

Cars crushed as trees fall by the score

By MIRROR REPORTER

Tribute to a sleeping giant . . .

CLAIM – AND MAKE IT SNAPPY!

You'll be at the back of the queue if you don't

By ROBERT HEAD, City Editor

EVENTS

Get your axe together

IF YESTERDAY's less extreme weather was anything to go by, the weekend will be the time for clearing up the mess left by Thursday night's storm. Advice from the professionals is that you should start repairing damage to trees today.

If a tree is past saving, it is best to saw it up immediately: green wood being much easier to cut. What may seem a massive task will be much simpler once you have stripped the smaller branches from a tree, and made a bonfire. Logs should obviously be cut to a length to fit your fire: if you wish to sell them they should not be longer than 18 inches. Ideally wood should be stored for a year before burning.

Many trees, even ones completely uprooted, can be saved. If no more than two major roots are broken, replant the tree, first cutting the broken roots neatly. When planting make sure earth is well-packed round the roots: there must be no air pockets. Place two stakes either side of the tree, two feet from the trunk, and nail a cross-bar between them. Tie the tree to the cross-bar with commercial plastic tie, available from any garden centre. Ordinary nylon will rot the bark.

Trees with branches torn away should be given first aid immediately. Trim the wound, and seal it with a pruning compound like Arbrex.

November-April is the time for re-planting, although container trees can be planted now. Many Garden Centres are open throughout the weekend — though in the South East much of their stock has been depleted. Stake your new tree well!

Information from Mount Harry Trees, Nr Lewes, E Sussex (0273-474456).

The Cost Of Clearing Up

Chain-saw hire: about £30 for the weekend. But shops we contacted on Friday said they had hired out most of their equipment already.

The professionals: Again, their services have been heavily booked. Most tree surgeons will give free quotes on the cost of heavy clearing or surgical work. Check under 'Tree Work' in the Yellow Pages, or choose a firm approved by the Arboricultural Association.

New trees: B&Q Garden Centres, with branches all over the South East, will sell you a seven foot potgrown Prunus for around £13. It will grow to some 30 feet in ten years. Acers (maples) for around £12-£15 are the fastest growing deciduous tree. Available from most tree nurseries.

If something like this is currently occupying your backgarden, the environmental pressure group Common Ground have a number of suggestions for getting trees back where they belong: Don't give up on stumps out of the ground, dig them in, trim them, and hope for new growth next year. Collect acorns, conkers and other fruits, germinate them and plant in the spring. Write to your local council or MP; show them you care that trees in your area are saved or replaced.

The devastating effect of the storm upon the landscape in the south east of England was thoroughly reported upon, photographed and analyzed by the national and local newspapers. Its effects were assessed and many helpful points were made for action by the decision-makers for the future of our countryside.

THE INDEPENDENT

MONDAY 19 OCTOBER 1987

NEWSPAPER
OF THE
YEAR AWARD

★★★ Published in London 25p

Insurers braced for welter of claims as policy-holders assess the impact of the hurricane

Gales ... flooding batter Britain

AS THE country began counting the cost of Friday's hurricane, gales and torrential rain yesterday lashed many parts which had escaped the brunt of last week's storms.

At least one person died yesterday. Wales and parts of northern England were under as much as six feet of water as rivers burst their banks, sweeping away cars and cutting off communities.

A man from Merseyside died in North Wales when he was caught in raging flood water during a climbing expedition in the mountains near Aber. He was named last night as Donald Morgan, from the Wirral.

Welsh firemen dealt with hundreds of emergency cal...

... without power yesterday because of the hurricane, despite ... al teams of en... ...inds

...ing the path of Friday's ...severe dam-

have to pay out around £4m. The main Commercial Union switchboard took 200 calls an hour, and Gengral Accident had a constant flow of inquiries.

that insurers would have to cover losses to growers worth £5m.

Commercial orchards were devastated by the winds and would take seven years to recover, Faith Tippett of the Women's Farming Union said. Her own farm in Essex lost between 500 and 700 apple trees.

...outh West was hit by ...0mph in places ...r roofs ...s fore-

...orlock, ...o which ...y's storm, ...y, but the ...aster, Da- ...een found.
...ects, page 2

New...

By David McK...
Ireland Corres...

SECURITY forces...

THE INDEPENDENT Monday 19 October 1987

PETER ALLEN

Pier pyre: Wreckage from the collapsed Shanklin Pier burning along with rubbish at t...

...lvaged useful timbers that were washed ashore.

Travellers warned

ALL OF BRITAIN'S main trunk roads, including motorways, were open last night, but the AA warned that expected heavy winds might bring down debris from weak...ned trees. British Rail expected that ...es would run on all main rout... ...the North, strong ...ng rain were ...ways, ...

...tes reopen

...providing only enough power to light the massive shed at their farm near Sheen, Hampshire, where the birds are housed.

"We are working 18-hour shifts to feed the chickens by hand," Mrs Gibson said. ...t's normally done by an electric feeder. ...ey need constant food, but no sooner ...e we filled up one trough and moved on ...e next than they've polished off the

...Gibson yesterday made a 240-mile ...ip to try to find another generator ...h to handle the feeding. ...ire dairy farmers poured hun- ...lons of milk down drains yes- ...se of the the power cuts. ...'s wife at Steep, Hampshire, ...er board for failing to sup- ...tions with emergency

...ting Board was refusing ...h could not be water ...egulations.

Looking down the scarp of White Hill, near Box Hill, Surrey, with its cover of Beech and Box. Before the storm (ABOVE) and after (BELOW)

ABOVE:
The Chile Pine or Monkey-puzzle tree. (*Araucaria araucana*). Since it was introduced to Britain from the Andes in the eighteenth century, this tree can often be seen in both large and small gardens.

ABOVE LEFT:
The beginning of Dutch Elm Disease infestation near Osterley Park in West London. Subsequently all the elms became victims of the disease

LEFT:
One of the beautiful sylvan scenes across the lake at the National Trust garden, Sheffield Park, Sussex

ground level, leaving what the Americans call a 'snag' standing. The lie of the land had some influence on the direction of the fall: most toppled downhill. But on south-facing scarps trees were first blown uphill by the force of the wind, only to slither butt-first downhill again.

Though it is the fallen trees which are the most noticeable, the most widespread damage was the loss of branches on the crowns of trees which remained standing. Some exposed trees had every branch ripped from them. Oddly, branches often succumbed to a twisting motion rather than a simple break. This left many branches ready to fall – the classic widow-makers.

Throughout the path of the storm the damage was patchy. Some areas of Kent had scarcely a tree damaged, whereas in other districts the trees were devastated. In the Sevenoaks area at Toys Hill it was an astonishing sight, with extensive mature beechwoods uprooted like fallen ninepins, with only ten per cent remaining standing. Similar devastation occurred at Slindon and West Dean in Sussex, Oaks Park in Surrey, and in many other places, including the commons in London. Remarkably, trees on the windward edge of London often survived, while those in the supposedly protected centre were blown down.

The Forestry Commission estimates that 15,000,000 trees were either destroyed completely or severely damaged.

Although this was a storm almost without precedent in Britain there were storms in central and south-west Scotland in 1953 and 1968 with winds reaching hurricane force, but the damage was trivial by comparison. However, in 1708 a storm killed 8000 people in the south of England.

How long will it take to clear up this tangled mess? The Royal Parks were cleared of fallen trees by the spring of 1988, but it will take at least five years to salvage the timber from plantations and woodlands, and some will just be left to rot. Replanting of the lost roadside trees will take at least three years, and parks should be restocked in the next five to ten years. Commercial plantations may be replanted in five years, but many woods will be left to regenerate naturally from seedlings or coppice shoots, and this will take longer.

Ecologically, the effects will last much longer than that. In 200 years' time in woods which are left to recover naturally, it will be possible to identify a generation of trees which date from just after the storm.

The great storm was certainly a disaster to those whose property was damaged, or who lost trees which were important to them. Certainly, too, many landscapes have suffered severe changes, not for ever, but for longer than our lifetimes. Ecologically, though, it may have some unexpected benefits, as flowers appear in the new clearings and other wildlife thrives upon the dead wood and the thickets which will develop.

STRESS, PESTS AND DISEASES

Stress

Plants have evolved mechanisms which enable them to adapt to and survive many fluctuations in the conditions of their particular habitat. In general terms stress may be considered as a severe disturbance, either temporary or fatal, to the metabolism of a plant. One of the most common stresses is of course water loss and the desiccating effect of dry air. Should the loss of water vapour through transpiration exceed the supply of water obtained from the roots, the plant will wilt and may ultimately die.

Areas of low rainfall may occur in both warm and cold climates, and prolonged periods of drought may occur even in equable temperate regions. Where average rainfall is low, extended periods of drought can have a catastrophic effect on the vegetation.

Plants have adapted to control their water content. They can reduce the exposed area of their leaves by controlling the guard cells around the breathing pores or stomata. In some plants, excessive sunlight may scorch their leaves, and they have developed a modification which allows them to flutter or adopt an orientation away from the rays of the sun.

The absorption of toxins, such as heavy metals, from the soil will produce stress in a plant which will stunt or distort its growth, and can frequently kill it. Heavy metals may occur naturally in some soils but, today, are occurring more frequently as a result of pollution.

The most controversial pollutant in relation to trees is airborne – acid rain. Acid rain is formed of a combination of sulphur dioxide and nitrogen oxide, emitted principally by power stations and cars. These gases go through a complex series of changes in the atmosphere to become sulphuric and nitric acids, and they fall back to earth as acid precipitation and acid dust.

For many years West Germany and the Scandinavian countries have complained that emissions from Britain and the countries of central Europe have been polluting their forests and lakes. In West Germany it is estimated that no less than fifty per cent of their trees are dead or dying, and that this figure will reach at least eighty per cent by the end of the century.

Surveys undertaken by the Forestry Commission in 1984 and 1985 reported that they could find no evidence of acid pollution causing damage to trees in Britain. Further research into this problem is now being undertaken for the Nature Conservancy Council by the Natural Environment Research Council.

On the face of it, and in the light of the European studies, it seems incontestable that the increasing acidification of the rainfall is at least one factor in the well-attested acidification of lakes across northern Europe. The more contentious issue is the extent to which acid rain is the cause of tree decline. If Britain's emissions of the ingredients of acid rain are indeed affecting northern Europe, then it is inconceivable that they are not also polluting our own rivers, lakes and woodlands.

Britain's Environment Minister stated in June 1988 that agreement had been reached by the EEC committing member countries to reduce sulphur dioxide emissions by 60% of the 1980 level by 2003.

Pests and diseases

Pests are organisms which feed upon the structure of a plant, while diseases are due to pathogens, organisms which, in addition to feeding upon the tissues, cause a breakdown of the healthy plant tissue.

Pests have evolved to exploit a niche in the natural world. Examples are the herbivorous caterpillar feeding on leaves, sap-suckers, and the beetle grub, which feeds on decomposing wood. There is a fine balance between pests, their food supply and their own predators. Many population fluctuations occur within a single season, and from year to year. However, the predators – hunting birds and larger insects – tend to keep local pest invasions in check. It is seldom that pests will completely destroy a food plant. Such an event is likely to be dependent on population density of the pest.

For example, a pest like the locust may reach plague proportions, or a disease strain may sweep through a hitherto unaffected population. Examples of the latter in this country are the Chestnut Blight and Dutch Elm Disease. Over the years, Dutch Elm Disease has been a greater destroyer of trees even than the great storm of 1987. The disease has been known since the early nineteenth century. There was a decline in the elm population during the 1920s and, by the 1930s, the disease had become widespread, but many of the trees affected by the fungus survived the attack.

In the late 1960s a more virulent form, imported from North America, struck British elms. At that time the population of elms was estimated at 22,000,000. By the mid-1970s over five million had succumbed and, today, a conservative estimate of the destruction is eighty per cent of the total population – about seventeen point six million elms: more than the total number of trees estimated to have been destroyed by the great storm.

The tree is an active organism with a renewable protective cover. The waxy cuticles and raised bark serve to insulate the delicate tissue of leaf, cambium and fruit from the adverse effects of the environment. Small injuries may be healed by callous growth. However, there is always danger from broken branches due to the action of animals or wind, permitting the entry of pathogens before healing can take place. Fungi, for instance, are always seeking fresh food supplies to colonize, and damp or damaged wood is readily invaded.

Monocultures of any plant, whether

grass, herb or tree, offer special opportunities for population explosions of particular pests, due to the abundance of the food supply. Pests have a fast rate of reproduction, and there may not be enough predators to have a significant effect on them. Similarly, a strain of a disease may become rampant very quickly throughout an entire monoculture.

The loss of leaves due to early frost, prolonged drought or defoliating insects may not kill a tree, and in following seasons it may regain its former strength again. Significant leaf loss will, however, prevent the tree from producing carbohydrates by photosynthesis and, once the reserve of sugars and other nutrients is exhausted, then the tree will die.

FIRE AND BROWSING

Although fire can be very destructive to trees and their associated shrubs and herbaceous plants, it has, paradoxically, an important role in the regeneration of natural forests. Clearance by fire aids the development of young saplings, the ash contains nutrients which assist in the growth of the emerging plants. For instance, the giant redwoods of California are very seldom blown down, and hence the only places in which their saplings can obtain the light they need to develop is in clearances created by fire. In fact, their seeds have evolved in such a way that they actually need fire in order to germinate.

In Britain, spontaneous fires are caused by lightning, which occasionally destroy trees and their shrub layer beneath. But these are few compared with the deliberate, controlled burning of the heather moors, which are called 'muirburns' in Scotland. The deep mats of heather and bilberry need to be cleared periodically to allow improvement of the soil and germination of the seeds. However, such fires have a habit of going out of control when a sudden change of wind direction coincides with a change of wind speed. Two years ago just such a mishap occurred on a National Nature Reserve in Galloway, when the fire burned for eight hours – causing serious damage both to the Reserve and to adjacent private and Forestry Commission plantations.

Heaths which are colonized by birch and pine are frequently destroyed by recurrent fires. Mainly natural, but occasionally due to human carelessness, they sweep across the heaths in dry summers. Birch will recolonize these areas rapidly and in great numbers, as their seeds are light and numerous.

Over-grazing is an important factor inhibiting the growth of natural woodland. Although this threat was greatly reduced when the rabbit population was reduced by myxomatosis, there is some evidence of a revival.

Browsing is another cause of destruction. The Red Squirrel (*Sciurus vulgaris*) is a forestry pest of some importance in the Highlands of Scotland and, despite efforts to reduce their numbers, they still remain plentiful. The Grey Squirrel (*Sciurus carolinensis*), which was introduced into Britain at the beginning of this century, has now become an established member of our fauna. Grey Squirrels have spread rapidly almost everywhere in England apart from East Anglia and the Isle of Wight, where the Red Squirrel still survives. Their destructiveness to trees and shrubs was soon realized. However, despite the numbers shot by farmers, gamekeepers and foresters, they are still maintaining their population increase, though in the 1930s there was a decline in numbers, possibly caused by a disease.

Reafforestation in the Scottish Highlands has been responsible for the spread of the Pine Marten, *Martes martes*, and, as squirrels and small rodents are important to their diet, their spread may prove to be beneficial to trees.

The most conspicuous browsers in Britain are the deer. Scottish Red Deer, *Cervus elaphus*, the largest species of deer in Britain, are naturally forest animals. They are particularly destructive to trees during the winter months, when they descend from their summer haunts to the valleys to feed upon bark, twigs and acorns. The Roe Deer, *Cervus capreolus*, is a native deer with a wide, though localized, distribution. It causes considerable damage to young plantations by rooting up seedlings and saplings with its antlers. The Fallow Deer, *Dama dama*, is not a native, but is widely if sparsely distributed throughout Britain. It too, through being destructive to both crops and plantations, is a serious pest to farmers and foresters. There are other species of deer which have escaped from parks and gardens and adopted a semi-wild life. If their populations increase they will pose a further threat to natural vegetation.

THE SITUATION WORLDWIDE

The decline of forests is not just a national problem: it is global. At the present time the Earth is the only known planet to contain a life-supporting system. Yet this capacity is being relentlessly impoverished, so threatening the very means on which life depends.

Until recently, the forests of the temperate zones of the world were in an apparent state of balance, due to efficient economic management and conservation policies. Now, a new threat has entered the arena – acid rain. Acid rain is posing a serious threat not only to the health of trees in West Germany, Poland, Bohemia, Scandinavia and Scotland, but also to aquatic flora and fauna.

But it is the tropical rain forests throughout the world which are causing the greatest concern to conservationists. These areas contain the Earth's most complex and species-rich communities. Unfortunately they are the most vulnerable to exploitation, due to the demand by the major consumers of the developed world for their valuable timber. This pressure on the forests, together with the poverty of the people farming these areas, threatens the very existence of the rain forests.

Some of the most vulnerable forests are not expected to survive beyond the turn of the century. A continuous supply of timber could be achieved if a sustained resource-management policy was adopted. Such a policy would safeguard the future of the vast populations of animals and plants, and would also mean survival for the indigenous peoples who live in harmony with nature, which is under threat.

Cutting wood for fuel and shifting cultivation in arid and semi-arid regions and in the rain forest areas are further threats to these sensitive ecosystems. Shifting cultivation is practised by the poor of undeveloped countries. There is no alternative if they are to survive in the present economic and food situation. Scrubby bushes and trees are felled or burned to clear the land so that crops can be planted. In the arid and semi-arid regions overgrazing by cattle, combined with occasional drought, causes the soil to be un-

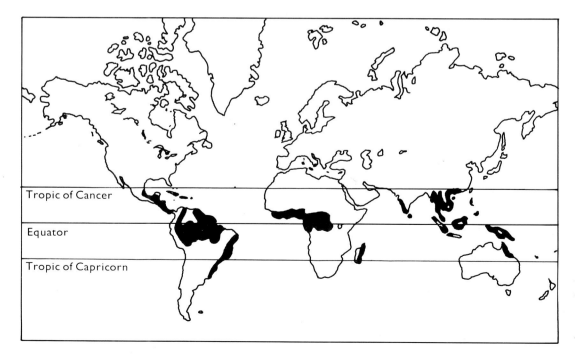

Distribution of tropical forests. Many of these are tropical rain forests – the most sensitive ecosystems in the world – and under threat of extinction.

stable and the topsoil is blown or washed away. The consequence is that more land has to be cleared and the process begins anew. Mali, in north-west Africa, provides an excellent example of this: over the last twenty years the Sahara Desert has advanced 300 miles into the country.

In the Amazonian regions populations have been moved into tropical rain forest areas to relieve the exploding populations in the cities. Generally, the soils of the rain forests are shallow and their fertility is low due to the rapid decomposition of the leaf litter. Hence only a few crops can be harvested from the cleared plots before it should lie fallow to regain its fertility. However, due to the desperate need for food for their starving families, the fallow periods become shorter. Then the soils become impoverished and less productive; the inevitable occurs, and further inroads into the forest are made. The topsoil of the abandoned ground is washed away into the streams and rivers during the tropical rains. It causes siltation, which reduces the flow of water and necessitates costly dredging operations to free waterways.

If this plundering of the world's resources is to be halted, then positive action by governments and non-governmental organizations, including industry and commerce, must be combined to implement the recommendations of the World Conservation Strategy and the aims of the Brundtland Report. These reports offer a framework and guidance for the necessary conservation measures. They emphasize the need for global co-ordination and concerted action to implement sustainable resource-development programmes.

CONSERVATION AND REGENERATION CONCLUSIONS

The traditional British landscape in both the lowlands and highlands is a mosaic of many different types of terrain and vegetation, in large part reflecting the uses to which it has been put by man over the millennia. Once it was covered almost entirely by natural forest. Very little, if any, of this original woodland exists today, and what does remain is semi-natural. Some of this type of woodland, which may not have been exploited directly by man but has been grazed by his livestock, may have been in continuous existence since Pre-Boreal times 10,000 years ago.

The hallmark of ancient woodland is its under-storey. If there is a wide variety of spring flowers, such as wood sorrel, wood anemones, primroses, bluebells and a good carpet of dog's mercury, which are all plants that do not thrive on disturbed ground, then the woodland is old.

The trees of our semi-natural woodland are an essential component of Britain's natural beauty, and they are also an important natural resource. Yet this resource, outside the protected areas, is at great risk. There is now a need to secure the survival of the original semi-natural woodland that remains, rather than to promote large plantations of introduced conifers.

The Nature Conservancy Council has been undertaking a census designed to produce, for each county or district, a list of all ancient and semi-natural woodlands, and those which have been planted. Shortly it hopes to have completed draft inventories for the whole country. Such information will be invaluable, to both governmental and non-governmental organizations, in identifying and protecting a complete representative selection of our native woodland.

Since Britain became a member of the EEC, there has been a large increase in the acreage of arable land. One of the many consequences of this has been the 'grubbing up' of hedgerows to facilitate ploughing, and this has reduced wildlife habitats. Another adverse effect is the loss of topsoil through wind erosion. The pattern of the countryside in East Anglia and the North and South Downs has been especially affected by this form of prairie-farming. The Downs were once almost a complete green sward, broken only by a profusion of chalk grassland flowers. Today it is a vast patchwork of brown and green.

The planting of serried rows of conifers over moorlands and mountainsides by the Forestry Commission and commercial syndicates has greatly reduced the variety of landscape as well as the wildlife interest. Many of these areas were either mixed or broadleaved woodlands, and hence were more varied and beneficial to the flora and fauna. Although today about eight per cent of Britain is covered by trees, this figure disguises the fact that a high percentage of this coverage consists of introduced conifer plantations.

At the present time the afforestation of the Flow Country in Caithness and Sutherland is a cause of special concern among conservationists. The Royal Society for the Protection of Birds in particular has strongly condemned the decision to plant a further 162,000 hectares (400,000 acres) of conifers. This area consists of blanket bogs or flows, and it is probable that it has never in the past had any tree cover. It is an area of international importance for breeding waders and waterfowl, including divers, greenshanks, golden plovers and dunlin.

On the credit side, an announcement has recently been made that the RSPB, supported by the NCC and the National Heritage Trust, has purchased the Abernethy Forest Estate in the Scottish Highlands. The area measures 7700 hectares (19,025 acres) and includes mountains, moorland and ancient pine forests. The aim of the Society is to allow the regeneration of the pine forest up to the natural tree line, so securing the habitat for the capercaillie, crossbill and crested tit. The reserve will be open to visitors.

Nonetheless, we are losing our traditional countryside at an unprecedented rate.

A further threat to individual trees and woodland in Britain happened in March 1988. Tree Preservation Orders have for some years been available to local Authorities to assist in making provision for the preservation of trees and woodlands. They are widely used and prohibit felling and other forms of destruction unless the authority gives its consent. Such orders apply both to trees in private gardens and in woodlands. The following case involving the Canterbury City Council was the subject of a recent High Court decision, and is in the latter category.

In 1983 a farmer sought permission from the Council to grub out about sixteen hectares (thirty-nine acres) of coppice woodland for agricultural purposes. The application was refused, and an ap-

peal to the Secretary of State was turned down in 1984. But in June 1986, a Tribunal awarded substantial compensation to the farmer based on the value of the land had it been converted to arable use. The Council appealed, but was rejected.

This outcome is causing considerable concern among local authorities and environmental organizations. Faced with the possibility of sizeable claims for compensation, it may be difficult for authorities to make Tree Preservation Orders or to refuse applications for consent to clear woodland. Unless some immediate action is taken to counteract this type of judgement by Government, a further threat to trees and woodlands throughout Britain will ensue.

There are, however, some encouraging signs of change in official attitudes. The Forestry Commission, for one, now has a definite conservation policy. Its two main aims for nature conservation are:

– to safeguard and, where practicable, to improve its woodlands as wildlife habitats
– to give particular attention to those sites where nature conservation has been identified as of special importance

It is encouraging too that, despite the vast and accelerating rate of the destruction of natural woodland that has taken place during and since World Wars I and II, there are now many organizations involved with the conservation of nature.

It is impossible to write about the conservation of trees without considering the role of the Forestry Commission. From its inception in 1919 its aim was to establish a strategic reserve of timber. Under the Forestry Act of 1967 it is charged with the general duty of promoting the interests of forestry, the development of afforestation and the production of forest products in Great Britain. In addition, under the Countryside Acts, it must 'have regard to the desirability of conserving the natural beauty and amenity of the countryside'. The Commission manages a substantial broadleaved estate which is located mainly in the lowlands of southern England, where the objective is to maintain the predominantly broadleaved character of the landscape. It works in close liaison with the Nature Conservancy Council and the County Naturalists' Trusts.

Since the Forestry Commission is the largest landowner in Britain, it has, over the decades, attracted a good deal of criticism. However, much of it, especially that to do with their plantations of monotonous regiments of conifers with little wildlife interest, is now no longer justifiable.

The Nature Conservancy Council is the government body which promotes nature conservation in Great Britain. It is concerned also with the establishment of National Nature Reserves, which in 1987 totalled 214, covering 155,419 hectares (384,050 acres). The two hundredth NNR was Cragbank Wood, one of the largest fragments of ancient broadleaved woodland remaining in the Scottish Borders – an area which has lost almost half its natural woodlands since 1947.

In addition to NNRs, the Nature Conservancy Council designates Sites of Special Scientific Interest which, up until March 1986, totalled 4842 sites covering 1,430,866 hectares (3,535,670 acres).

There has been over the last decade a considerable growth in the number of organizations involved in the varied aspects of nature conservation. The County Trusts in particular deserve mention. Among other tasks they establish and manage Local Nature Reserves. One particular recent coup, in 1987, was the acquisition by the Dorset County Trust of a large part of the unspoilt Lower Kingcombe Farm, West Dorset.

The recent accelerating decline in native woodlands could begin to be reversed over the next decade with the release of land from intensive agriculture. This opportunity has arisen as a result of the EEC's attempts to curb the production of surplus cereals. Some of the land so released should be allowed to regenerate naturally, and some should be managed back to a woodland state by the planting of native trees.

Although we can derive satisfaction from the close liaison between the governmental conservation and forestry organizations and the non-governmental societies, we should not allow ourselves to become complacent. Much effort is still needed to ensure the future of Britain's native woodlands: despite the receding of the threat from agriculture, the demands of development on our limited resources of land will not diminish with time, but will diversify.

As individuals we may be able to achieve very little by way of influencing governmental and non-governmental decision-makers but, by joining one of the ecological societies, we can help to bring pressure to bear on officials to pursue more conservation-oriented policies.

A World Conservation Strategy was prepared in 1980 by the International Union for the Conservation of Nature, and states the principles for sustainable use and management of resources. This Strategy outlines the major conservation problems, along with suggested action and priorities. However, it could not be applied to problems at national levels. Thus, a Conservation and Development Programme for the United Kingdom has been prepared with the co-operation of the following organizations:

Man, Tree, Wheat. If the current rates of land degradation continues almost one-third of the world's arable land will be destroyed over the next twenty years. During the same period the productive tropical forests will be halved and some lost forever. At the same time the world's population is estimated to increase from just over 4,000,000,000 to almost 6,000,000,000.

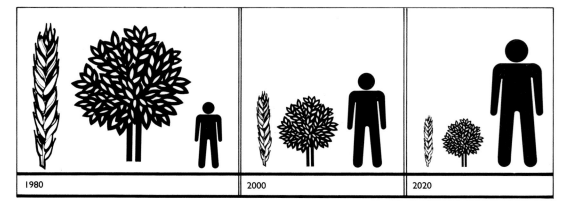

World Wide Fund for Nature
Countryside Commission
The Royal Society of Arts
Nature Conservancy Council
Countryside Commission for Scotland
Council for Environmental
    Conservation

Adapting the objectives of the World Conservation Strategy to meet UK conditions led to agreement that action was needed in the following three areas:

– the integration of conservation, with both the living and non-living resources, with development
– developing a sustainable society in which both physical and psychological needs are fully met
– developing a stable and sustainable economy through the practices of resource-conservation in all spheres of activity

While this Development Programme does outline in detail the areas requiring a conservation strategy, what is needed is continued impetus to promote the recom-

mendations contained within these reports, and support for the Programme in the future. What is most important is to encourage the British public to accept an active role and constructive participation in a UK Conservation Programme that affects our daily lives and future.

Britain has a long tradition of interest in the natural world and also for the preservation of her heritage. Nevertheless, greater efforts must be made to disseminate more information covering all things that affect the environment, through the variety of media now available.

On a world basis there is a need for action to apply the World Conservation Strategy, as rising human numbers and consumption are making increasing demands on the Earth's limited resources. This problem is illustrated opposite below. If the current rate of land degradation continues, then one-third of the world's arable land will be destroyed. Similarly, by the end of this century the productive area of tropical rain forest will have been halved. The world's population will have increased from 4,000,000,000 to almost 6,000,000,000 during this period.

NATURE CONSERVATION TRUSTS IN THE UK
Associated with the Royal Society for Nature Conservation (RSNC), and the National Association of Conservation Trusts

AVON
Avon Wildlife Trust
The Old Police Station,
32 Jacob's Wells Road,
Bristol BS8 1DR
Bristol 0272 268018/265490

BEDS & HUNTS
Bedfordshire & Huntingdonshire
Wildlife Trust
Priory Country Park,
Barkers Lane,
Bedford MK41 9SH
Bedford 0234 64213

BERKS, BUCKS & OXON
Berkshire, Buckinghamshire and
Oxon Naturalists' Trust, (BBONT)
3 Church Cowley Road,
Rose Hill,
Oxford OX4 3JR
Oxford 0865 775476

BIRMINGHAM
Urban Wildlife Group (Birmingham),
(UWG)
131–133 Sherlock Street,
Birmingham B5 6N8
Birmingham 021 666 7474

BRECKNOCK (Brecon)
Brecknock Wildlife Trust,
Lion House,
7 Lion Street,
Brecon, Powys LD3 7AY
Brecon 0874 5708

CAMBS/ISLE OF ELY
Cambridgeshire Wildlife Trust,
5 Fulbourn Manor,
Manor Walk, Fulbourn,
Cambridge CB1 5BN
Cambridge 0223 880788

CHESHIRE
Cheshire Conservation Trust,
c/o Marbury Country Park,
Northwich,
Cheshire CW9 6AT
Northwich 0606 781868

CLEVELAND
Cleveland Nature Conservation Trust,
The Old Town Hall,
Mandale Road, Thornaby,
Stockton on Tees,
Cleveland TS17 6AW
Stockton on Tees 0642 608405

CORNWALL
Cornwall Trust for Nature
Conservation,
Dairy Cottage, Trelissick,
Feock, Truro,
Cornwall TR3 6QL
Truro 0872 862202

CUMBRIA
Cumbria Trust for Nature
Conservation,
Church Street,
Ambleside,
Cumbria LA22 0BU
Ambleside 0966 32476

DERBYSHIRE
Derbyshire Wildlife Trust,
Elvaston Castle Country Park,
Derby DE7 3EP
Derby 0332 756610

DEVON
Devon Trust for Nature Conservation
35 New Bridge Street,
Exeter,
Devon EX3 4AH
Exeter 0392 79244

DORSET
Dorset Trust for Nature Conservation
39 Christchurch Road,
Bournemouth,
Dorset BH1 3NS
Bournemouth 0202 24241

DURHAM
Durham County Conservation Trust,
52 Old Elvet,
Durham DH1 3HN
Durham 091 386 9797

DYFED
Dyfed Wildlife Trust,
7 Market Street,
Haverfordwest,
Dyfed SA61 1NF
Haverfordwest 0437 5462

ESSEX
Essex Naturalists' Trust,
Fingringhoe Wick Nature Reserve,
Fingringhoe, Colchester,
Essex CO5 7DN
Rowhedge 020628 678

GLAMORGAN
Glamorgan Wildlife Trust,

Nature Centre,
Fountain Road,
Tondu,
Mid Glamorgan CF32 0EH
Bridgend 0656 724100

GLOUCESTERSHIRE
Gloucestershire Trust for Nature
Conservation,
Church House,
Standish, Stonehouse,
Glos GL10 3EU
Stonehouse 045 382 2761

GUERNSEY
La Société Guernesiaise (LSG)
c/o Dr T N D Peet,
Le Chêne, Forest,
Guernsey C. I.
Guernsey 0481 38620

GWENT
Gwent Wildlife Trust,
16 White Swan Court,
Church Street,
Monmouth,
Gwent NP5 3BR
Monmouth (9am–1pm) 0600 5501

HANTS & ISLE OF WIGHT
Hampshire & Isle of Wight
Naturalists' Trust,
8 Market Place,
Romsey,
Hants SO5 8NB
Romsey 0794 513786

HEREFORD & RADNOR
Herefordshire & Radnorshire Nature
Trust,
Community House,
25 Castle Street,
Hereford HR1 2NW
Hereford (am only) 0432 56872

HERTS & MIDDX
Hertfordshire & Middlesex Wildlife
Trust,
Grebe House, St Michael's Street,
St Albans,
Herts AL3 4SN
St Albans 0727 58901

KENT
Kent Trust for Nature Conservation,
The Annexe,
1a Bower Mount Road,
Maidstone,

Kent ME16 8AX
Maidstone 0622 53017/59017

LANCASHIRE
Lancashire Trust for Nature
Conservation,
The Pavilion,
Cuerden Park Wildlife Centre,
Shady Lane,
Bamber Bridge, Preston,
Lancs PR5 6AU
Preston 0772 324129

LEICESTER & RUTLAND
Leicestershire & Rutland Trust for
Nature Conservation,
1 West Street,
Leicester LE1 6UU
Leicester 0533 553904

LINCS & STH HUMBERSIDE
Lincolnshire & Sth Humberside Trust
for Nature Conservation,
The Manor House,
Alford,
Lincs LN13 9DL
Alford 05212 3468

LONDON
London Wildlife Trust,
80 York Way,
London N1 9AG
London 01 278 6612/3

MAN (ISLE OF)
Manx Nature Conservation Trust,
Ballamoar House,
Ballaugh,
Isle of Man
Sulby 062489 7611

MONTGOMERY
Montgomeryshire Wildlife Trust,
8 Severn Square,
Newtown,
Powys SY16 2AG
Newtown 0686 24751

NORFOLK
Norfolk Naturalists' Trust,
72 Cathedral Close,
Norwich,
Norfolk NR1 4DF
Norwich 0603 625540

NORTHAMPTONSHIRE
Northants Wildlife Trust,
Lings House,
Billing Lings,
Northampton NN3 4BE
Northampton 0604 405285

NORTHUMBERLAND
Northumberland Wildlife Trust,
Hancock Museum,

Barras Bridge,
Newcastle-upon-Tyne NE2 4PT
Durham 091 232 0038

NORTH WALES
North Wales Naturalists' Trust,
376 High Street,
Bangor,
Gwynedd LL57 1YE
Bangor 0248 351541

NOTTINGHAMSHIRE
Nottinghamshire Trust for Nature
Conservation,
310 Sneinton Dale,
Nottingham NG3 7DN
Nottingham 0602 588242

RADNORSHIRE
Radnorshire Wildlife Trust,
1 Gwalia Annexe, Ithon Road,
Llandrindod Wells,
Powys LD1 6AS
Llandrindod Wells 0597 3298

SCOTLAND
Scottish Wildlife Trust, (SWT)
25 Johnston Terrace,
Edinburgh EH1 2NH
Edinburgh 031 226 4602

SHROPSHIRE
Shropshire Trust for Nature
Conservation,
St George's Primary School,
Frankwell, Shrewsbury,
Shropshire SY3 8JP
Shrewsbury 0743 241691

SOMERSET
Somerset Trust for Nature
Conservation,
Fyne Court, Broomfield,
Bridgwater,
Somerset TA5 2EQ
Kingston St Mary 082345 587/8

STAFFORDSHIRE
Staffordshire Nature Conservation
Trust,
Coutts House, Sandon,
Staffordshire ST18 0DN
Sandon 088 97 534

SUFFOLK
Suffolk Wildlife Trust,
Park Cottage,
Saxmundham,
Suffolk IP17 1DQ
Saxmundham 0728 3765

SURREY
Surrey Wildlife Trust,
Old School,
School Lane,

Pirbright,
Woking,
Surrey GU24 0JN
Brookwood 0483 797575

SUSSEX
Sussex Wildlife Trust,
Woods Mill, Shoreham Road,
Henfield,
West Sussex BN5 9SD
Brighton 0273 492630

ULSTER
Ulster Trust for Nature Conservation,
Barnett's Cottage,
Barnett Demesne, Malone Road,
Belfast BT9 5PB
Belfast 0232 612235

WARWICKSHIRE
Warwickshire Nature Conservation
Trust, (WARNACT)
Montague Road,
Warwick CV34 5LW
Warwick 0926 496848

WILTSHIRE
Wiltshire Trust for Nature
Conservation,
19 High Street,
Devizes,
Wiltshire SN10 1AT
Devizes 0380 5670

WORCESTERSHIRE
Worcestershire Nature Conservation
Trust,
Hanbury Road,
Droitwich,
Worcestershire WR9 7DU
Droitwich 0905 773031

YORKSHIRE
Yorkshire Wildlife Trust,
10 Toft Green,
York YO1 1JT
York 0904 659570

RSNC
Royal Society for Nature
Conservation, (RSNC)
The Green,
Nettleham,
Lincoln LN2 2NR
Lincoln 0522 752326

CONSERVATION CONTACTS

Arboricultural Association,
Ampfield House,
Ampfield, Romsey,
Hants SO5 9PA
Romsey (0794) 68717

Birds of Prey Conservation Centre,
Leighton Hall,
Carnforth,
Lancashire

Birds of Western Palearctic,
Stanley Cramp,
71 Gray's Inn Road,
London WC1

Botanical Society of the British Isles,
c/o British Museum (Natural History),
Cromwell Road,
London SW7 5BD
01-589 6323 x 701

British Association for the Advancement of Science,
Fortress House, 23 Saville Row,
London W1X 1AB
01-734 6010

British Association of Nature Conservationists,
c/o Rectory Farm,
Stanton St John,
Oxford OX9 1HF

British Bryological Society,
A R Perry,
Department of Botany,
National Museum of Wales,
Cardiff CF1 3NP

The British Butterfly Conservation Society,
Tudor House,
Quorn, Loughborough,
Leicestershire LE12 8AD
Loughborough (0509) 42870

The British Deer Society,
The Mill House,
Bishopstrow, Warminster,
Wiltshire BA12 9HJ
Warminster (0985) 216608

British Hedgehog Preservation Society,
Knowbury House,
Knowbury, Ludlow,
Shropshire

British Herpetological Society,
136 Estcourt Road,

Woodside,
London SE25 4SA

British Lichen Society,
c/o Department of Botany,
British Museum (Natural History),
Cromwell Road,
London SW7 5ED

British Mycological Society,
c/o Department of Plant Sciences,
Wye College, Nr Ashford,
Kent TH25 5AH

British Trust for Conservation Volunteers,
36 St. Mary's Street,
Wallingford,
Oxford OX10 0EU
Wallingford (0491) 39766

British Trust for Ornithology,
Beech Grove, Tring,
Hertfordshire HP23 5NR

Civic Trust,
17 Carlton House Terrace,
London SW1Y 4AW
01-930 0914

Civic Trust for Wales,
St Michael's College,
Llandaff,
Cardiff CF5 2YZ
Cardiff (0222) 552388

CLEAR
9 Northdown Street,
London N1 9BG

CoEnCo (Council for Environmental Conservation),
Zoological Gardens, Regent's Park,
London NW1 4RY
01-722 7111

Conservation Action Project,
Peak National Park Study Centre,
Losehill Hall, Castleton,
Derbyshire S30 2WB
0433 20373

The Conservation Foundation,
Aviation House,
129 Kingsway,
London WC2B 6NH
01-242 4637

The Conservation Society,
12a Guildford Street,
Chertsey,
Surrey DT16 9BQ

The Conservation Trust,
246 London Road,
Earley, Reading RG6 1AJ
Reading (0734) 663650

Council for National Parks,
4 Hobart Place,
London SW1W 0HY
01-235 0901

Council for the Protection of Rural England,
4 Hobart Place,
London SW1W 0HY
01-235 9481

Country Landowners' Association,
16 Belgrave Square,
London SE1X 8PQ

Countryside and Heritage Presentation Group,
25 Glenmore Road,
Salisbury,
Wiltshire SP1 3HF
0722 24519

Countryside Commission,
John Dower House,
Crescent Place,
Cheltenham,
Glos GL50 3RA
0242 21381

Earthlife Foundation Ltd,
37 Bedford Square,
London WC1B 3HW

Economic Forestry Group,
Forest House,
Great Haseley,
Oxford OX9 7PG
Great Milton (08446) 571

The Exmoor Society,
Hoar Oak House,
Alcombe,
Minehead,
Somerset

Farming and Wildlife Advisory Group,
The Lodge,
Sandy,
Bedfordshire

Fauna and Flora Preservation Society,
Zoological Gardens,
Regent's Park,
London NW1 4RY
01-586 0872

Field Studies Council,
62 Wilson Street,
London EC2A 2BU
01–247 4651

Field Study Centre (Badgers),
Laughter Hole Farm,
Postbridge, Yelverton,
Devon
Tavistock (0822) 88265

Friends of the Earth,
26–28 Underwood Street,
London N1 7JQ
01-490 1555

The Geologists' Association,
Dept of Geology,
University College London,
Gower Street,
London WC1E 6BT

Greenpeace,
30–31 Islington Green,
London N1 8BR

The Hawk Trust,
Loton Park, Shrewsbury,
Salop
Shrewsbury (0743) 78232

Heritage Wildlife Rescue,
11 Elm Drive,
Middleton-on-Sea,
West Sussex PO22 6JB

Institute of Terrestrial Ecology,
Monks Wood,
Abbots Rippon,
Huntingdon PE17 2LS

International Council for Bird
Preservation,
219c Huntingdon Road,
Cambridge CB3 0DL
Cambridge (0223) 277318

International Dendrology Society,
Whistley Green Farmhouse,
Hurst, Reading,
Berkshire

International Union for Conservation
of Nature and Natural Resources,
219c Huntingdon Road,
Cambridge CB3 0DL
Cambridge (0223) 277314 and 277420
(Species Conservation Monitoring
Unit) and 277427 (Wildlife Trade
Monitoring Unit)

Jersey Wildlife Preservation Trust,
Les Augres Manor,
Trinity, Jersey,
Channel Islands
0534 61949

Kent Farming and Wildlife Advisory
Group,
15 Manor Road,
Folkestone CT20 2AH

Landmark Trust,
Shottezbrooke,
Maidenhead,
Berkshire
Maidenhead (0628) 82341

Linnean Society of London,
Burlington House,
Piccadilly,
London W1V 0LQ

London Wildlife Trust,
1 Thorpe Close,
London W10 5XL
01–968 5368/9

The Mammal Society,
c/o the Linnean Society,
Burlington House,
Piccadilly,
London W1V 0LQ

Men of the Trees,
7 Abbotsfield Crescent,
Tavistock,
Devon PL19 8EY

National Association for
Environmental Education,
Perry Common School,
Faulkners Farm Drive,
Erdington,
Birmingham B23 7XP

National Trust,
36 Queen Anne's Gate,
London SW1H 9AS
01–222 9251

National Trust for Scotland,
4 Charlotte Square,
Edinburgh EH2 4DU
031 226 5922

Natural Environment Research
Council,
Falcon House,
Swindon,
Wiltshire
Swindon (0793) 26231

Nature Conservancy Council,
Northminster House,
Peterborough PE1 1UA
Peterborough
(0733) 40345

The Otter Trust,
Earsham,
Bungay,
Suffolk

Peak National Park Study Centre,
Losehill Hall, Castleton,
Derbyshire S30 2WB

People's Trust for Endangered
Species,
19 Quarry Street,
Guildford,
Surrey GU1 3EH
Guildford (0483) 35671

Ramblers Association,
1–5 Wandsworth Road,
London SW8 2LJ
01–582 6878

Royal Entomological Society,
41 Queen's Gate,
London SW7 5HU
01–584 8361

Royal Forestry Society,
102 High Street,
Tring,
Hertfordshire HP23 4AH
Tring (044282) 2028

Royal Scottish Forestry Society,
18 Abercromby Place,
Edinburgh EH3 6LB
031 557 1017

Royal Society for Nature
Conservation,
The Green, Nettleham,
Lincoln LN2 2NR
Lincoln (0522) 752326

Royal Society for the Prevention of
Cruelty to Animals,
The Manor House,
The Causeway, Horsham,
Sussex RH12 1HG
0403 64181

Royal Society for the Protection of
Birds,
The Lodge,
Sandy,
Bedfordshire SG19 2DL
Sandy (0767) 80551

Royal Society of Arts,
8 John Adam Street,
London WC2N 6AJ
01–839 2366

Save Britain's Heritage,
3 Park Square West,
London NW1 4LY
01–486 4953

Scottish Civic Trust,
24 George Square,
Glasgow
041 221 1466

Scottish Field Studies Association,
Kindrogan Field Centre,
Enochdhu,
Blairgowrie,
Perthshire PH10 7PG
Blairgowrie (0250) 81286

Scottish Wildlife Trust,
29 Johnstone Terrace,
Edinburgh EH1 2NH
031 226 4602

The Soil Association,
86 Colston Street,
Bristol BS1 5BB

Tradescant Trust,
St Mary's Church,
Lambeth,
London SE1

The Tree Council,
35 Belgrave Square,
London SW1X 8QN
01–235 8854

The Tree People,
89 Charlton Park,
Midsomer Norton,
Bath,
Avon

Trees for People,
71 Verulham Road,
St Albans,
Hertfordshire AL3 4DJ

Trust for Urban Ecology,
c/o the Linnean Society,
Burlington House,
Piccadilly,
London W1V 0LQ
01–734 5170

Urban Wildlife Group,
11 Albert Street,
Birmingham B4 7UA

Watch,
22 The Green,
Nettleham,
Lincoln LN2 2NR

The Wildfowl Trust,
Slimbridge,
Glos GL2 7BT
Cambridge (Glos) (045 389) 333

Wildfowlers' Association of Great
Britain and Ireland,
Marford Mill, Rossett,
Clwyd
Rossett (0244) 570881

The Wildlife Rescue Service,
The Old Chequers,
Briston, Melton Constable,
Norfolk
Melton Constable
(0263) 860375

The Woodland Trust,
Westgate, Grantham,
Lincs NG31 6LL
Grantham (0476) 74297

World Society for the Protection of
Animals,
106 Jermyn Street,
London SW1Y 6EE
01–839 3026

World Wide Fund for Nature – UK,
Panda House,
11–13 Ockford Road,
Godalming,
Surrey GU7 1OU
Godalming (048 68) 20551

The XYZ Club,
(Young Zoologists Club),
London Zoo,
Regent's Park,
London NW1 4RY

Young Ornithologists' Club,
The Lodge,
Sandy,
Bedfordshire SG19 2DL

Young People's Trust for Endangered
Species,
19 Quarry Street,
Guildford,
Surrey GU1 3EH
Guildford (0483) 35671

The Zoological Society of London,
Regent's Park,
London NW1 4RY
01–722 1802/3333

GLOSSARY

Achene   A small, dry, one-seeded fruit from one carpel, which doesn't split to release the seed

Acuminate   Tapering to a fine point

Adpressed   Closely pressed, flat against the stem or root, pointing towards the tip, as in the scales of cypresses

Alternate   Not in opposite pairs on the same node

Angiosperms   True flowering plants that produce seeds enclosed in an ovary

Anther   The pollen producing terminal structure of the stamen

Arborescent or Arboreal   Of tree size and form

Aril   A fleshy, usually coloured growth from the stem which partially covers the seed, as in yews

Auricles   Small, paired lobes at the base of a leaf

Axillary   In the upper angle at the junction of a leaf stalk and the stem

Berry   A fleshy fruit without a stone but with embedded seeds

Bract   A modified leaf, usually green and scale-like, at the base of a flower

Bract-scale   A modified leaf that becomes a protective scale for seeds in a conifer cone

Calyx   Collective name for sepals of a flower

Capsule   A dry, dehiscent fruit that splits open to release the seeds while still on the tree

Carpel   One or more units of the female reproductive organs of the Angiosperm flower, each made up of the ovary containing one or more ovules

Clones   Plants derived vegetatively from cuttings, suckers or buds from a single parent tree

Columnar   Tall and narrow with parallel sides

Compound   *See* **Pinnate**

Cordate   The heart-shaped bases of leaves

Corolla   Collective name for the petals of a flower

Crown   Part of the tree formed by the branches and leaves

Cultivar   Abbreviation for 'cultivated variety'

Cupule   A cup-like structure holding a nut-like fruit, eg acorn and hazel

Decussate   Leaves in opposite pairs on a stem

Dehiscent   Dry fruits which split open to release their seeds, while still on the tree

Deltoid   Triangular leaves, with rounded lateral corners, eg some birch and poplars

Digitate   Leaves that radiate from a central point like spreading fingers, eg Horse Chestnut

Dioecious   Male and female flowers on separate trees

Drupe   A fleshy fruit with a hard stony shell containing one seed

Epicormic   Arising from dormant buds on the trunk or older branches

Epiphyte   A plant growing on another plant, but not parasitic on it

Fastigiate   Almost erect branches, eg Lombardy Poplar

Genus   A natural group of closely related species which have certain characteristics in common

Glabrous   Without hairs

Glaucous   With a grey-blue or white bloom

Gymnosperms   Flowering plants whose flowers are unisexual. Conifers are the most important group.

Hybrid   Offspring of different species or varieties of plants

Indehiscent   Fruits which do not open to release their seeds, but are shed complete with their seeds

Inflorescence   A natural arrangement on a plant of individual flowers on the same stem

Laciniate   Leaves cut into long narrow lobes by deep incisions

Lanceolate   Spear-shaped

Lateral   From the midline or axis to the flanks

Lenticels   Pores on the bark of a tree, which allow gaseous exchange between the atmosphere and the tissues of the tree, ie 'breathing'

Lobe   A segment of a leaf, divided from adjacent segments by sinuses or incisions

Midrib   Central axial vein of a leaf of a broadleaved tree

Monoecious   Bearing male and female flowers on the same tree

Node   The point where a leaf or leaves originate

Oblique   A leaf with unequal or asymmetrical base

Opposite   Leaves arranged in opposite pairs on the same node of a stem

Ovary   The basal part of the carpel of an Angiosperm flower, in which the ovules develop

Ovate   Egg-shaped with variations

Ovule   The egg or female reproductive structure of the ovary which contains the female sex cell

Ovuliferous   The egg-bearing scales that develop in the axils of the bract scales of conifer cones

Panicle   A branched inflorescence in which the flower stems branch from common stalks

Peltate   The scales of globose cypress cones

Perfect   Flowers containing organs of both sexes

Perianth   The calyx and corolla collectively

Pericarp   The outer wall of the ovary after it has matured into a fruit

Petiole   The stalk of a leaf

Pinnate   Having two rows of appendages on each side of a common stalk

Pistil   The female organs of a flower

Raceme   An inflorescence of stalked flowers borne on a common stalk

Rachis   The common stalk of an inflorescence or a compound leaf

Samara   A dry indehiscent fruit with a flat leathery or horny capsule

Sepal   An individual segment of the calyx, the outer envelope of a flower

Sessile   Without a stalk

Species   A natural group of organisms that are essentially similar

Spike   A simple inflorescence with stalkless flowers on a common stem

Spur   A short segmented shoot or branchlet, usually bearing a whorl of leaves, a flower or a cone

Stamens   The male organs of a flower bearing the pollen producing anthers

Stigma   The pollen receiving female organs at the tip of a style

Stipule   A leafy appendage, sometimes scaly, at the base of the petiole bud-scale on some species of trees

Stomata   Pores in leaves which allow for gaseous exchange between the atmosphere and the tissues of the leaf

Strobilus   Botanical term for a conifer cone

Style   A thread-like extension of the ovary, which terminates in the stigma; absent in some flowering plants

Truncate   Sharply ending as if cut at the base

Umbo   The raised rough or spiny centre of the scale-end of a pine cone, usually tipped with a spine

Whorl   A ring of three or more branches or leaves, borne at the same level on the parent axis

BIBLIOGRAPHY

Clapham, H R, & Nicholson, B E, *The Oxford Book of Trees* (Peerage Books, 1973)

Clapham, Tutin & Warburg, *Flora of the British Isles* (University Press, 1968)

Cronquist, A, *Introductory Botany* (Harper & Row, 1971)

Fleure, H J, 'Natural History of Man in Britain', *New Naturalist* (Collins, 1970)

Fraser Darling, J, & Morton Boyd, J, 'The Highlands and Islands', *New Naturalist* (Collins, 1969)

Godwin, Sir Harry, *History of British Flora*, 2nd edn, (CUP, 1975, paperback 1984)

Hart, C, & Raymond, C, *British Trees in Colour* (Michael Joseph, 1973)

Hora, Bayard, Ed, *The Oxford Encyclopedia of the Trees of the World* (Peerage Books, 1986)

Johnson, Hugh, *The International Book of Trees* (Mitchell Beazley, 1973)

Lawrence, Eleanor, Ed, *The Illustrated Book of Trees and Shrubs* (Octopus, 1985)

Lowson, J M, *Textbook of Botany* (University Press, 1940)

Martin, Elizabeth, *Trees of Britain and Europe* (Kingfisher Books, 1978)

Mirov, Nicolas, *The Story of Pines* (Indiana University Press, USA, 1976)

Mitchell, Alan, *A Field Guide to the Trees of Britain and Northern Europe* (Collins, 1974)

Mitchell, Alan, *The Trees of Britain and Northern Europe* (Collins, 1982)

Nature Conservancy Council, The *Nature Conservation of Great Britain* (NCC, 1984)

Nature Conservancy Council, The *Annual Report* (NCC, 1986)

Nimmo, Derek, *The Illustrated Encyclopedia of Trees* (Leisure Books, 1978)

Pennington, Winifred, *The History of British Vegetation*, 2nd edn, (English University Press, 1974)

Pokorny, Jaromir, *Hamlyn Colour Guides to Trees* (Hamlyn, 1987)

Swinnerton, W H, 'Fossils', *New Naturalist* (Collins, 1969)

Tansley, A G, *Britain's Green Mantle* 2nd edn, revised by Michael Proctor (Allen & Unwin, 1968)

Tebbs, Barry, Ed, *Trees of the British Isles* (Orbis, 1984)

Wilkinson, Gerald, *A History of Britain's Trees* (Hutchinson, 1981)

Wilkinson, Gerald, *Epitaph for the Elm* (Hutchinson, 1978)

World Conservation Strategy, *International Union for the Conservation of Nature and Natural Resources* (Gland, Switzerland, 1980)

ACKNOWLEDGEMENTS

We are most indebted to many of our past colleagues for their valuable help. We would especially like to thank Dr George Peterken of the Nature Conservancy Council, David Burton of Strathclyde County Council, Douglas Scott for his draughtsmanship, and Michael Copus for permission to use his painting of the British landscape during Carboniferous times. We are also most grateful for the assistance given by Dr B Burbidge of the Royal Botanical Gardens, Kew, and by Clive Jermy of the British Museum (Natural History), and to the National Trust at Polesden Lacey for granting facilities to photograph fallen trees in their gardens.

Finally, our acknowledgements cannot be complete without thanks to William Facey, for his swift and indefatigable editing work and valuable contribution to the organization of the text.

INDEX

Page numbers in italic refer to illustrations

PICTURE CREDITS

All photographs are by Eric Herbert, apart from the following:
Michael Copus 23; Clive Jermy 38 (below).
Syd Lewis's drawings are on 11, 14, 15, 17, 19, 20 (above, below), 73, 104
The publisher and authors would like to thank the Glasgow Geological Museum for the photograph on 21.
Newspaper extracts on 108–9 are by permission of The Daily Mirror, Syndication International and The Independent, Newspaper Publishing plc.